Little America

Rob Swigart

CORONET BOOKS
Hodder and Stoughton

D1324575

Printed and bound in Great Britain for
Hodder and Stoughton Paperbacks, a
division of Hodder and Stoughton Ltd,
Mill Road, Dunton Green, Sevenoaks, Kent
(Editorial Office : 47 Bedford Square,
London, WC1 3DP) by William Collins
Sons & Co Ltd, Glasgow

ISBN 0 340 22959 4

From Karl & Charles & Sigmund & Albert & most of all Werner Heisenberg, whose Uncertainty Principle is a metaphor with punch:

> ... we can no longer ignore the physical processes through which we obtain our knowledge ... We can no longer speak of the behaviour of a particle independently of the process of observation ... When we speak of the picture of nature in the exact science of our age, we do not mean a picture of nature so much as a picture of *our relationships with nature.*
>
> – *The Physicist's Conception of Nature*

& of course from Sophocles, who was probably the first man to have scrawled on the rest-room wall of a tavern somewhere under the Acropolis the ultimate truth:

OEDIPUS REX WAS A MOTHERFUCKER

though we will never know for certain.

Prologue

Wheels: it might be said that the universe invented wheels to keep itself rolling – great round galaxies turning through the dark, and suns themselves turning, and around them the planets, and on the planets the circles of weather and currents and rocks rolling downhill, and tumbleweed rolling; perhaps also the universe itself a giant wheel unreeling the indelible tread of photons as it rolls from then to now, from beginning without beginning to end without end over the icy black highway of intergalactic nothing; perfect wheels without any need of steering or brakes, only slowing slowly as the inconceivable driverless truck comes down off the gradient and coasts for its eons across the tedious Great Plains of Ultimate Entropy.

And if he had been born at another time, or the great Wheel of Karma had zigged instead of zagged, Orville Hollinday would not, perhaps, have been born into a nation of wheels on a world of wheels. He would not, perhaps, have been born a self-aware, featherless biped destined to spend a statistically significant portion of his life cycle inside capsules that rolled on wheels over endless interconnected ribbons of asphalt, concrete, tarmac, from here to there and back again, in a universe that rolled on and on, though it knew in the tiny decaying orbit of every improbable electron and meson and quark that somewhere the wheel would slow to a stop, but that when it did the universe would collapse and explode and start rolling again, because it is in the nature of wheels to roll.

He might, instead, have been born an ant-eater, say, or a jackrabbit hopping cutely across the open land near Interstate 80, his little fuzzy flag of a tail quivering and flashing in the golden late afternoon sun that sent his bounding shadow streaming out across the brown land. He might hop unknowing towards the highway where the cosmic wheel of an enormous west-bound semi, driven by one Arthur Henley, forty-one years old, with a wife and five children in Orlando, Florida, and the sun in his eyes, might flatten him forever with a tiny, uncosmic pop, only to send him rolling into another cycle of the endless

7

wheel, this time as a whooping crane or a slow loris, or a Siamese twin or a saint, a philosopher, a king.

Arthur Henley himself has rolled across this featureless landscape more times than he can remember, and will continue to do so, unaware of that *bump bump bump bump* as the jackrabbit that might have been Orville Hollinday is rolled wafer-thin by the huge tyres of his truck, which carries a load of electronic sensing devices, thermocouples, microwave generators, Geiger counters, readouts and telltales destined for a Methane-Cooled Slow-Burn Breeder Reactor in Idaho belonging to the company founded by Orville's Uncle Wilbur. Arthur Henley is troubled somewhat by his haemorrhoids, itching madly down there at the end of the looping yards of his ample intestines, and is anxious to reach Little America, Wyoming, the world's largest service station, for a hot shower and a cold beer after all those aching bumpy miles from Orlando, Florida, so he stayed unaware that the jackrabbit's skinny remains stuck fast to his left rear-most wheel like the chalk mark of some cosmic meter maid. It will fall off when he reaches Little America anyway.

But Orville wasn't that jackrabbit; he was born instead, fully human, into the twentieth century to a mother who loved him and a father who didn't, and he had to make his own way to Little America.

1

'Your son,' Orville on the other side of the sliding doors to the living-room heard his father say to his mother the summer he was sixteen, 'is a cissy. Your son,' Orville felt his father's voice as though it were an unripe lemon being squeezed into a series of small lacerations up his spine, 'is a *little* cissy. A *short*, little cissy.'

Orville leaned against the wall in the darkened hallway a few feet from the front door. The glass panes on either side of the door filtered in some watery porch light, and distorted squares of light fell on the silvery-blue walls and the antiqued blue-and-white table, above which the gilt-framed mirror bounced back at him his feeble outline. I'm not *that* short, he thought.

His parents were fighting in their restrained, well-bred way, there in the cool green living-room, the green accented with blue, so hall and living-room flowed in co-ordinated colours from one to the other. At least that's what the man his father called 'the dancing decorator' had said.

Orville was a disappointment to his father. Besides being too short, he couldn't shoot a gun, he didn't like to hunt, he never made a team, he read a lot of books. He was working this summer stamping the prices on canned vegetables at the supermarket, but his father thought he ought to be out doing construction work.

I'm not that short, he thought again. I'm as tall as the manager, and he's not that short. And he's older. He walked unsteadily to the double doors to listen to the argument.

'Your kid is a little nothing,' he heard his father saying. His father was a kindly bespectacled man with an air of irrefutable logic, unruffled calm and superior efficiency that did nothing to conceal his mean streak. 'I don't know why you indulge him like that.' And Orville, listening, began, despite his protestations to himself, to shrink. He lost an inch just realizing that to his father he was only his mother's son. 'I mean, *encouraging* him to work in a supermarket.' Two more inches melted from

Orville's stature.

'He ought to be doing a man's work. Construction, that's what he needs. Something to toughen him up. Jesus Christ, little cissy.' These last muttered words dripped hot disgust on Orville's melting size.

'Now, Senior, leave the boy alone. He got the job himself.' His mother's voice was mild, and Orville knew she was looking down at her soft white hands folded in her lap, two meek lambs of the Lord lying down with the lion.

'Bullshit! You shop there all the time. They know you. You got him that goddam job!' Senior's voice notched up another dB, and dwarfish Orville teetered on a razor of rage and fear outside the door, his tiny mis-shapen body quivering in a silent hum too high for the human ear, for now his mother too is threatened.

'Senior, please. He'll hear you. He's only sixteen.'

'He's only sixteen.' Senior's voice spread with a thick lard of sarcasm that sent the frequency of tiny Orville's vibration up another octave, so in the darkness of the hall his outlines began to blur, and his twisted form began to oscillate back and forth, a wider swing each time, until at last he swirled down the enormous drain of his rage and fear.

'That Orville is a runt,' his father began to rant, when the doors suddenly slammed open and Orville lurched and waddled through, his eyes spinning in his wrinkled, atavistic face in search of a lethal weapon.

Unfortunately the only thing that midget Orville could see that he could reach was his mother's favourite Wedgwood lamp standing on the authentic walnut table next to the sea-green couch, its Wedgwood blue harmonizing decorously, so said the dancing decorator, with the green of the sea of the couch.

The nymphs and shepherds in sharp ceramic white lounged around the lamp's plump belly, all singing together in a subtle noontime harmony of leisure and lust, and even when Orville seized the lamp and brandished it above his head before swinging it, a medieval mace, at his black knight father, the nymphs and shepherds showed no surprise.

From shrimpy Orville's squeaky throat a screeching bellow wavered into whispers. He swung the lamp and swung the lamp, and his father's startled face swelled and shrank in Orville's still turbulent eyes, and then he swung with all his might at the rapidly changing target in front of him, and with a terrible soundless bellow the pastoral nymphs and shepherds, still singing their pursuit, veered away from Senior's balding head at the last moment and crashed awfully down on Orville's own head, which stood exactly five feet ten inches above the foamy off-white deep-pile carpet of that oceanic living-room.

When he woke up in the hospital he realized he'd always wanted to kill his father.

2

'I'm going to kill that son of a bitch,' said Orville. He was lying on top of Mary Lou Perkins in the back seat of his 1958 Edsel convertible. Both he and Mary Lou were eighteen years old, and neither one of them knew quite what to do there in the back seat, but Orville had a terrific hard-on, and Mary Lou didn't seem to mind.

'Gee, Orville, who are you going to kill?' she asked in a voice that sounded as if she were thinking of something else.

Though neither one of them was aware of it, the Edsel looked out on one of the most beautiful prospects that their midwestern city could afford them: the entire town was lit up like Christmas, giving an eerie flickering loveliness to the undersides of the greasy industrial clouds that hovered like guardian angels only a few hundred feet above their heads. Orville couldn't see it because he was thinking in a furious murderous rage about killing his father; and Mary Lou couldn't see it because Orville's chin blocked out everything else.

'Who are you going to kill?' she vaguely encouraged again, distracted as she was by the slow grinding of Orville's hips and the peculiar warmth this was producing in her groin.

'I'm. Going. To. Kill. My. Father.' Orville said through tightly clenched teeth. His left foot kicked involuntarily against the back of the front seat like a frog leg on a galvanometer, knocking it into the steering wheel. The shock clicked the Edsel into Neutral. Imperceptibly the car began to glide down the slight slope of the parking lot that offered the finest view of Eden Park, so that gradually the twinkling panorama of city and river slid downward off the windshield, leaving only the faintly luminous sky there. Neither Orville nor Mary Lou noticed.

'When I was sixteen he told my mother I was too short once too often,' Orville went on, the pace and ferocity of his grinding hips increasing exponentially. 'I tried to kill him then, but something happened to stop me. Damn!'

'I don't think you're too short,' panted Mary Lou, who was four-foot-eleven, the shortest girl in Orville's high school class. But she was as cute as a pair of Capezio's and a circle pin, and she lived two blocks away from Orville, who was still a virgin, though a high school graduate.

Patrolman Hiram Quint, in his squad car parked in the darkest pool of shadow in the entire parking lot, did not notice the 1958 Ford Edsel convertible moving slowly and silently backwards down the gradient towards him. Patrolman Quint cared nothing then for patricidal rage, because he was crouched under the dash shining his flashlight on the pages of a dirty comic book one of the other patrolmen had seized during the arrest of a seventy-seven-year-old man who had been trying to sell them surreptitiously on Vine Street between coughs.

Patrolman Quint was just reaching tentatively for his fly, his eye intently focused on the page, the flashlight clenched under his chin to leave his hand free, when there was a long, almost placid sound of rending metal as the Edsel, having reached a maximum speed of seven miles per hour, cruised dreamily backwards into the left rear door of the squad car.

'I'm . . . gonna . . . kill . . .' Orville was saying, his groin and Mary Lou's groin colliding violently in a frenzy like two antelope stags in rut, as at the exact moment of impact he exploded with terrific force into his Fruit of the Loom boxer shorts that had been laundered fresh that very day by his mother's loving hands, '. . . son of a bitch.'

'Gee, Orville,' said Mary Lou.

3

Orville dreamed from living-room to ambulance to hospital of going to Little America and having his own gas pump.

'Little America?' his father screamed when Orville told him

from his hospital bed. 'Where the hell is Little America?'

'It's in Wyoming.' Orville's head bobbed its enormous halo of soft white bandage up and down. 'It's the largest gas station in the world. Over a hundred pumps.'

Orville's father thought his son was crazy. He walked fiercely out of the room into the corridor smelling of disinfectant and buttonholed the psychiatrist who had examined his crazy son. 'He ought to be committed,' he told the psychiatrist.

The psychiatrist, a remarkably thin man who smoked a large meerschaum pipe which he continually tamped down with a long hairy finger, a finger that scurried in and out of the bowl like a furry snake going in after a gopher, disagreed.

'Your son is quite sane,' he told Senior with an authority Senior believed in without question, since he was a man who knew nothing of the workings of the human heart, though he knew a hell of a lot about money, which was a great deal more important.

'He's rational and relatively stable; he can do quite complicated mathematical procedures in his head,' the psychiatrist, Dr Schmidlapp, was saying. 'We'll have to do some further tests to discover why he had that sudden aberration yesterday, but I suspect there may have been some provocation.' Dr Schmidlapp's finger slithered into the bowl of his pipe.

'This could have been a neurotic symptom, or it could have been a part of normal adolescent rebellion.' The finger slithered back out.

'But frankly, Mr Hollinday, your son just doesn't seem to like you very much.'

'What do you mean? He hit himself on the head, not me.' Senior was puzzled.

'Mmmm. Yes,' said Dr Schmidlapp, and excused himself. Senior promptly forgot what he'd been told.

He was to spend the rest of that summer preparing Orville for college. He never mentioned the incident with the lamp, in part because he simply didn't believe it was really an attack on *him*. He thought it was just some peculiar self-destructive urge of Orville's.

'You're going to Harvard,' Senior told his son. 'The best. You will major in Accounting and Russian. We have to understand those people if we're going to beat them. Economics is going to be the battlefield. That's where we have to be prepared to fight them.'

Orville's adviser in college told him he had no real aptitude for Accounting, but he studied hard and graduated in the exact middle of his class. Orville hated his father, but he was also scared to death of him.

'Don't you understand,' Senior told the psychiatrist later on. 'He wants to go to some place called Little America and have his own gas pump.'

'It is not crazy, in the clinical sense, merely to desire something other people don't,' said Dr Schmidlapp icily. He peered into his meerschaum's bowl and nodded, then started flapping at his pockets in search of a match. Then he told Senior about Oedipus.

'I don't know anything about that,' said Senior. 'I'm a business-man.'

In his hospital room Orville's mother sat by his bed holding his hand and moaning over and over, 'Oh, Orville, Orville.' She was a very attractive auburn-haired lady who was famous in her circle for her salads and the methodical organization of her house. Orville, through a haze of pain in his head, never once thought she might be moaning over the loss of her lamp, its nymphs and shepherds swept forever into the trash.

Orville only knew that she was the most beautiful, warm-hearted, kind, sensitive, loving woman in the world, and cer-tainly the only person he would ever want to marry.

4

'What I'm going to do when I get out of here,' Orville told his room-mate at Yale Law School one night when the two of them had been smoking a generous amount of Acapulco gold Orville had scored in downtown New Haven. 'What I'm going to do . . .'

There was a long silence, broken into smaller silences by the slow but fascinatingly relentless dripping of the kitchen faucet. The silence, Orville noticed, lasted an entire lifetime. In fact, the silence between drips lasted an entire lifetime, each drip punctuated the end of a life, each drip punctuated especially the end of his father's life, and Orville fell with each drop into the profound timelessness of each moment, and felt with an almost unbearable pleasure the sharp thunder of each murderous globule of water crashing into the cranial ceramic of the sink.

'Yeah?' said Bert Flynn, his room-mate, whose mind had been marching to a different tune all this while, a tune never to be heard by the rest of the universe, but recalled at long last to a New Haven present in which Orville had begun a sentence.

'What I'm going to do when I graduate from Yale Law School,' Orville began again. Orville's father had insisted that he attend law school, and had, in fact, helped out when it was discovered that Orville's grades at Harvard were not really the sort of grades that Yale felt its freshmen law students ought to have to be real Yale men. After the establishment of the new Orville Hollinday Senior Chair of Business Rhetoric at Yale, however, Orville Hollinday, Junior, had no trouble becoming a Yale-trained lawyer.

'Orville,' Orville Senior, whom everybody called 'Senior,' said to his son, 'you must go to law school, and you must concentrate on International Business Law, for that is the only way we can beat those Russians at their own game. Unless we can bleed their economy until it's white instead of red, ha-ha, they'll be over here before you know it, buying up everything we have. Or taking it.' Senior's sense of humour veered towards the primitive.

So Orville went to Yale Law School, where he concentrated on International Business Law, and where he learned that practically speaking there was no such thing.

'What I'm going to do when I leave this place,' Orville began again, 'is to move out West where men are men.' He didn't notice any echoes of his father's manner of speaking, but eyed Bert instead. Bert, six-foot-five, stretched out full-length on the imitation Persian rug that came with the apartment. 'I'm going to LA,' Orville finished with an air of triumph.

'Yeah,' said Bert, getting into it. 'Hollywood and Vine, Sunset Strip, teeny-boppers, Homes of the Stars.'

'Not that LA,' said Orville without rancour, lost in his dream. 'Little America. Wyoming. The world's largest service station, over a hundred pumps. Restaurants, showers, dozens of restrooms, novelty stands, electric shavers . . .' His voice trailed off, overcome by the grandeur of it. 'My own pump, premium and regular, four hoses, two on each side, a niche for myself, better than that supermarket I worked in when I was sixteen.

'Maybe even,' he said, daring really big now, 'maybe even my own service *island*.'

5

'My own island,' Orville was saying to Private First Class Martin Freebnik as the two of them worked side by side cleaning the grease traps of the huge US Army stoves in the mess hall of Company B. Everyone called Pfc Freebnik 'Eggs', because of the enormous numbers he ate every morning at breakfast. This was, in fact, one of the main reasons Pfc Freebnik was now cleaning the grease traps; his habit had finally irritated Sergeant Laurel, the cook.

The world was not yet terribly frightened of cholesterol, so Pfc Freebnik didn't know how lucky he was to be exercising so hard, breaking down the massive quantities of animal fat he had been packing into his arteries. Even when the world did care about such things, Pfc Freebnik didn't. It caught up with him forty-six years, four months and six days later in the middle of a Spanish omelet.

'Yes, sir, my own island. Four pumps, *sixteen* hoses, a rack for oil, windshield wiper solvent, anti-freeze.' Later he would want to add a pump for low-lead.

Orville was drafted into the army right out of law school. Because he had a law degree, knew accounting, and could speak fluent Russian, and because he had connections, the army made him a specialist in Atomic Weapons Technology.

There was a war going on at the time, and most of the young men drafted into the army, and that was almost all of them, were shipped overseas to be chopped into small pieces, usually by American warplanes, shooting what was called 'friendly fire'. The enemy had the good sense to stay out of the way most of the time, leaving the Americans no one to practice on but themselves. Orville's high school class had been pretty much eliminated in this way. Even Mary Lou Perkins's twin brother Frank had returned from overseas in a much-decorated plastic bag the year after Orville and Mary Lou had been arrested for assaulting a police officer with a 1958 Ford Edsel convertible, light blue in colour, with dark blue vinyl upholstery, classified in Officer Quint's report as a 'deadly weapon', since it had truly

16

scared the shit out of him.

Orville's Uncle Wilbur had arranged for his nephew to stay in the United States, where he could damage the war effort as little as possible. Uncle Wilbur manufactured a small part for jet engines. It cost him twenty-seven cents to make each one; he sold them to the Pentagon for three dollars and fifty-nine cents each. He sold millions of them. He explained the discrepancy by telling the Pentagon that they were made from a titanium-platinum alloy; no one ever bothered to check and find out that they were really made from a tin-iron alloy that worked *almost* as well. Uncle Wilbur was a lot better at accounting than Orville.

Uncle Wilbur called up his golfing buddy and prime contact at the Pentagon, General Richard 'Dick' Carter, and told him about Orville.

'Dick, my nephew Orville would like security clearance and an important job. He's a bright boy if a bit of a fuck-up, so see what you can do.' General Carter, who fully expected to become president of Wilbur's firm after his retirement, promised he'd get right on it.

'What the hell you want to do that for?' asked Pfc Freebnik, who also had some connections. He scowled at a bit of egg yolk that had floated down into the grease trap he was cleaning. What a waste.

'It's my dream. Little America for life, the heart of the nation, crossroads of the world. That, and to kill that son-of-a-bitching father of mine.'

Basic training had given Orville some grand ideas.

6

Senior was a happy man. Sometimes he would step outside his office on the ground floor of the headquarters building of Hollinday Industrial Pharmaceuticals Inc. and gaze across the landscaped grounds of the industrial park at the huge smoke-stacks of his plant. He would muse on the rich beauty of the thick black smoke that rose, on a day like this, straight up like the Pillars of Hercules to merge with the almost solid roof of cloud overhead. Yes, he would think, it holds up the world.

Today, however, he didn't even glance at the smoke. He paced to and fro on the patio of his office, whistling to himself. The little twit had gotten in!

'Miss Freemont!' he snapped in the direction of the hidden microphone. Immediately his secretary's voice came back from the hidden speaker. 'Yes, sir.'

'Get my wife on the phone.'

'Yes, sir.' Miss Freemont couldn't keep the surprise from her voice. Senior never talked to his wife when they were in the same room, much less over the phone.

A brief G-major progression told Senior his call was ready. He went inside and picked up the phone. 'Hello. The little asshole got in.'

'What's that? Senior? Is that you?'

'Yes, it's me. The little asshole got into Yale. It took some doing but we got him in. Do you understand? The little asshole . . . got . . . in!'

'What little asshole, dear?' Mrs Hollinday was busy sewing name tags into Orville's underwear. She had turned out in front of her the waistband of the very pair of shorts that had been so gloriously and tragically despoiled with Mary Lou Perkins, so she was having trouble understanding what her husband was telling her. It was Flora Hollinday's supreme pleasure to sew name tags into her son's underwear. She positively doted on him; he was her true joy in life, after her husband, of course. She often missed Senior's references to 'that little piece of shit' or 'the little asshole'. Anything Orville did was fine with Flora.

Nothing Orville did was fine with Senior. 'Orville, you little . . .' Senior almost said 'You little asshole' to his wife, but he was feeling too fine and proud of himself to be harsh, so he ended it, 'piece'.

'Oh. Orville. Why that's fine, dear. He'll be going away again, and he'll need these labels I'm sewing in his underwear.'

'Yes, indeed. Maybe that little jerk will turn into something yet.' Senior leaned back in his seven-hundred-and-fifty-dollar executive chair and gazed almost fondly through the sliding glass door of his office at the plastic geraniums swaying gently in the breeze. 'Ah, yes,' he said gently to himself, as though he had already forgotten he held the phone in his hand, 'that little twerp will be the death of me yet.'

18

7

Orville found himself alone on guard duty in the Bomb Room. He had just relieved his best buddy in the Second Platoon, Company B, Private First Class Martin 'Eggs' Freebnik, who was also an Atomic Weapons Technology specialist, and he was marching smartly counterclockwise around the room, stopping momentarily at each corner as ordered.

The room was a vast cinder-block shell, nearly empty, with I-beams supporting a ceiling lost in darkness. Only a small video monitor near the one door, the three enormous pallets in the centre of the room holding the three Big Bombs, and Orville occupied all those echoing spaces. The door was securely locked from the inside, and no one else could enter the room without first announcing the code words for the evening through the intercom and showing identification and a signed pass to the video scanner outside the door.

On the door a label identified the building as US ARMY AGRI-CULTURAL HOLDING STATION, SECTION FOUR, NUTS AND FRUITS. The label fooled no one, and everyone on the base called it the Bomb Room.

Orville marched solemnly around the room four times, stopping at attention at each corner and executing a smart left face before marching on. Then he sat down and stared into the gloom near the ceiling. The only lights in the room were three huge banks of fluorescents that dangled a few feet above the three Big Bombs. The bombs were named Big Momma, Big Daddy and Wee Wee. These names had been painted in large letters in international orange on the sides. General James J. Schmidlapp, a distant cousin of the psychiatrist who had tested Orville when he was sixteen, thought the names were very cute. 'Good for morale,' he told his executive officer one night at the officers' club. General Schmidlapp was the base commander.

Orville had always been curiously drawn to Big Daddy, the middle of the three Big Bombs, which were all exactly alike, old-fashioned fission devices, rather larger than the newer models. But to Orville Big Daddy, with its commanding central position, Authority flanked by Duty and Respect, seemed somehow more powerful, more awesome. When he was on duty during the day with the other members of his unit of Atomic Weapons Technology specialists, polishing the bombs' brass fittings or servicing their important parts, testing the circuits of the timing mechanisms and so forth, Orville had pretty much marked out Big Daddy as his special project.

After staring at the ceiling for a few moments, as though lost in thought, Orville got up and walked unsteadily over to Big Daddy. This was the first time he had been alone on guard duty in the Bomb Room, and the time was ripe.

He was very familiar with the bomb's anatomy. In the back, near the guidance vanes, was a hexagonal nut set into the body of the bomb about three inches. Behind this nut, which was approximately one and one half inches in diameter, was a tunnel that led into a pool of machine oil which Big Daddy could draw on when operational to lubricate his mechanical parts.

Taking the proper tool from the rack under the bomb, Orville carefully removed the nut, leaving open an eight-inch tube straight into the body of the bomb.

He then took a tube of grease from the rack, and with mounting excitement coated the inside of the tube with it.

And then he undid his pants and with a strange, demonic gleam in his eye he screwed the brains out of Big Daddy.

He did that every month for eighteen months, leaving an enormous pool of sperm floating in Big Daddy's lubrication reservoir.

8

Orville's first job when he got to Little America was working on the lube rack. One day, when Orville had been there about six months, Charles 'Chuckie' Chipwood, who owned the Li'l Injun gas concession at Little America, removed the tiny plastic earphone from his right ear long enough to voice his agreement that Orville seemed to know quite a bit about lubrication.

'Dodgers four, Giants two,' he said. 'I don't unnerstand how some little eastern pissant can know so much about lubrication.'

He put the earphone back in without waiting for his second-in-command, Arnold 'Slim' Piggot, to reply. Slim was from Rock Springs, Wyoming, and had followed Horace Greeley's advice and moved thirty-eight miles west to Little America to find opportunity.

'Said he learnt about it in the *army*,' Slim answered anyway. He always answered his boss, even though Chuckie never heard. It was the bottom of the ninth, and Chuckie was rooting for the Giants.

Slim always pronounced the word 'army' as though it were in italics. He had a vast respect for anyone who had gotten near the killing. A trick elbow from high school football had kept him out, though he had begged the recruiter in Rock Springs for the chance.

The two of them were leaning against the Coke machine in the grimy Li'l Injun office, gazing through the open door to the garage where Orville worked his ass off greasing a 1973 Cadillac Coupe de Ville with twenty-three hundred miles on it. The owner was over in the Silver Dollar Café trying to cajole a waitress named Florence Biedernick into giving him a blow job. So far it had cost him ten cups of coffee and the nerves in his neck were beginning to jangle.

He would be unsuccessful, and would drive nine hundred and seven miles straight through that night to a motel on the outskirts of Salem, Oregon, where he would call up an old high school girl-friend, now married with six children. She would rush right over and oblige him, for old times' sake.

Chuckie and Slim knew nothing of Orville's ambition to eventually own his own gas concession in Little America. They would have been appalled at the grandeur of such an ambition. Chuckie owned the concession because he had answered an ad in the Billings, Montana, paper for someone to run the Li'l Injun franchise in Little America, Wyoming, and he thought that would be better than the job he had then been holding down for the past twelve years as an orderly in the Billings Hospital terminal kidney ward, where he emptied and cleaned the urine retention bags.

They certainly knew nothing of Orville's plans to do in his father. Orville had gotten cautious on that subject in the past few years. But as he squirted thick grease into the joints of that Cadillac Coupe de Ville, which was exactly the same kind of car his father drove, he hummed happily to himself. He knew

21

that eventually everyone in the United States, including Senior Hollinday, had to pass through Little America.

Orville was under the left rear wheel, just raising the grease gun, when he heard an enormous squealing of air brakes. He looked out under the Cadillac and saw a huge truck pull up to the diesel fuel pump.

On the side of the truck, in large letters, were the words RADIOACTIVE MATERIALS, and beneath them the yellow and violet on purple trefoil warning. The door opened and the driver of the truck swung down and stretched.

'Son of a bitch,' said Orville into the left rear wheel of the Coupe de Ville. 'That's my cousin Owen driving that truck!'

9

Orville's cousin Owen, Uncle Wilbur's son, was a tall, dark, good-looking boy who always got good grades and played folk songs on the guitar beautifully. At debutante parties all the loveliest girls followed him around in hopes that he would dance with them and perhaps even crush his delicious pubis forward into their crinolines. Orville thoroughly detested him.

They stood together in line at Bobo Winkler's coming-out party waiting to greet the hosts and tell them what a wonderful party it was and how extraordinarily glad they were that they had been invited and how original the decorations were and so forth. Owen would probably bend down and gallantly kiss Bobo's sweaty hand, and her mother would begin to feel a predatory glow flush through her stout torso. Unfortunately, Bobo had inherited her mother's torso and her father's nose.

'Great to see you again, Owen,' said Orville with as much conviction as he could muster. Owen had not been named Wilbur, Junior, the way Orville had been named Orville, Junior, because Owen's father hated the fact that Grandfather Hollinday had named his sons after the Wright brothers. Grandfather Hollinday had owned the bicycle rental concession in a park in Goshen, Indiana, in the early years of the century, and had deeply admired the Wright brothers for doing things with bicycles that he, Grandfather Hollinday, had never thought of doing. He thought the first names would inspire his sons to make something of themselves in the American way.

Orville's father had been called Senior long before Orville, Junior, was born. He was called Senior as soon as his younger brother Wilbur was born, something that Wilbur resented all his life. Wilbur never forgave Senior for being older, and favoured, and referred to as Senior, and often thought to himself when he was a boy that if he ever got the chance he'd like to kill his older brother. He never got the chance.

'Terrific to see you again, Orville,' said Owen. 'This looks like a terrific party, doesn't it?' Owen actually sounded sincere. He has the knack of sounding sincere, Orville thought. He also uses the word 'terrific' a lot.

'How's Uncle Wilbur,' Orville asked, just to keep the conversation going. The line inched forward through the splendid gold and white entrance hall of the country club, under the glaze of the crystal chandeliers, past the fluted wood columns wound with Christmas holly. It was two days before Christmas during Orville's senior year at Harvard, the Christmas that Orville received a brand-new 1964 Ford Falcon convertible to replace the Edsel he had wrecked with Mary Lou Perkins, who was not at the party tonight, but home with the flu.

'Dad's just dandy,' said Owen. He also said 'dandy' a lot. 'We're adding a whole new wing on to the bomb shelter.' Uncle Wilbur was one of the few people in the country who maintained his enthusiasm for bomb shelters into the nineteen sixties.

While Owen described in detail the cunning, space-saving tricks built into the new wing of the bomb shelter, Orville allowed his eyes to unfocus, and, in the distance, near the swarm of people around the bar, saw a vision of home-made bombs which blended with the glow he thought he would feel when he finally got to a place with over a hundred gas pumps.

10

'Why'd your Uncle Wilbur do that?' asked Bobalou Trbochet.

'He was afraid the Russians were going to bomb the city we lived in because of his factory. In the fifties he started manufacturing a small part for jet engines. He sold them to the Pentagon for slightly over one thousand three hundred per cent profit, and he was afraid the Russians might get wise to him. I don't know why he was afraid they'd bomb him because of that. You'd think they'd fall down laughing if they ever found out he was ripping off the Pentagon.'

'Wasn't he afraid the Pentagon would find out?' asked Bobalou.

'No. He had some dumb, powerful friends there.'

Orville and Bobalou were sitting in Bobalou's pale green 1974 Dodge van in the parking lot of the Crossroads Drive-In in Little America. It was the summer of 1975, and they were having Giant Bicentennial Burgers with Stars and Stripes Malteds. A Stars and Stripes Malted contained vanilla, blueberry and cherry ice-cream. The Crossroads Drive-In was feeling especially patriotic.

Bobalou had grown up on a farm near Long Prairie, Wyoming, which was not far from Little America. She had the largest, fullest, ripest, most gorgeous pair of lips Orville had ever seen, and she could do amazing things with them. She had the 5 a.m. to noon shift at the Li'l Injun station.

Bobalou placed the order of french-fried onion rings, called a General Lafayette, on the console between the seats. She had not yet eaten them; she had an idea for them for later.

Orville was so excited that all his plans were nearing fruition he barely tasted his Bicentennial Burger. He had recently joined the transcendental meditation study group in Little America, and he felt an unhurried calm about his plans. So he nodded attentively when Bobalou told him she thought building a bomb shelter was silly, that there were so many other more interesting things to do.

But Orville wasn't really listening. His attention was mainly riveted on the sight of her moist pink tongue nosing out of her mouth to flick the last vestiges of the Special Sauce from the corners of her incredible lips. She crumpled the paper wrappers of the Giant Bicentennial Burgers and dropped them into the trash bag under the dash. Then she began to shrug out of her grease-covered one-piece mechanic's jump suit, which she had bought at the general store in Granger for seventeen dollars. It was the same mechanic's uniform that sold at Bergdorf Goodman's in New York City for one hundred and fifty-five dollars.

Later Bobalou asked, 'Does he still have the bomb shelter?'

'No,' said Orville. He lay on his back on the imitation fur rug covering the mail-order water bed in the back of Bobalou's Dodge van. He'd thrown his pants in a heap near the back doors.

'After my last year at Yale Law School he went down into his bomb shelter to admire it again. This was in nineteen sixty-seven. For some reason the electricity wasn't working down there. He may or may not have noticed a funny smell – I guess he didn't. Anyway, he lit a match, and there was a gas leak, and his bomb shelter blew him to smithereens.'

'Oh God, how awful,' said Bobalou as she munched another onion ring off Orville's throbbing prong.

11

Flora Hollinday did not like fried foods in spite of the fact that her good friend Andrew Winkler owned a chain of fast food out-lets all over the Midwest called Kernel Korn's Drive-In Restaurants. Kernel Korn's speciality was deep-friend corn fritters on a bun with a Special Sauce. Mr Winkler was one of Hollinday Industrial Pharmaceutical Inc.'s best customers.

Flora was carefully poaching two eggs for her son Orville. She had waited patiently until she heard him stir, then tiptoed down to her all-electric kitchen to make his breakfast. It was one-thirty in the afternoon following Bobo Winkler's coming-out party, a party which, for discretion's sake, Flora had not attended. She and Andrew both were afraid they would lose their heads.

It was Christmas Eve.

Andrew had already called Flora from his office, however, to fill her in on the party, so she knew more or less what had happened, who had danced with whom, how long people had stayed, décor (which she had, in fact, helped to plan) and so forth.

'I understand your cousin Owen kissed Bobo Winkler's hand in the reception line last night,' she greeted Orville as he stumbled into the kitchen.

'Unh,' said Orville. He knew two poached eggs were steeping

25

in the saucepan on the stove, and his stomach began to crawl slowly towards his mouth.

'He certainly is *gallant*.' Mrs Hollinday said it with a French accent.

'Unh.'

The fact of the matter was that Owen had not only kissed Bobo's hand in the reception line, he had later slipped out the side door with her and done something vaguely thrilling and illicit on the eighteenth tee, in spite of her mother's torso and her father's nose. It was an experience that Bobo was to remember with secret shame and delight the rest of her life.

'I understand he even took her for a moonlight stroll on the golf course,' said Orville's mother, pushing firmly on the lever of the toaster.

'Unh,' said Orville. He knew perfectly well that even if there had been a moon last night it would never have pushed its way through the December cloud layer that still blanketed the city. Fortunately it had been unseasonably warm, though Owen was just thoughtful enough to have secreted his Yale football blanket nearby just in case.

'He told me he received a special scholarship to Harvard Law School,' said Orville. He didn't really care that Owen got a scholarship he didn't need, or that Owen had been accepted by the law school of his choice while Orville had not yet even heard whether Yale Law had received his application, but because his mother thought Owen was a real peach he always tried to say something nice about him.

12

Boy, that Owen is sure an asshole, Orville thought to himself as he watched his cousin stretch in his graceful, well-groomed way beside the cab of his huge diesel. But what the hell is he doing driving a truck? Owen had become president of his father's company after the bomb shelter blew up.

Owen waited patiently, and finally Slim Piggot detached himself from the Coke machine and strolled with a curious sideways roll to his hips to the gas pump. Slim always talked as though his walk were responsible for his getting laid on the average of twice a night by all the juiciest girls in Little America, but the fact was, the only girl to tolerate his advances at all was the deaf-mute who worked at the Taco House. Her extraordinary ugliness made the Taco House the least popular restaurant in the entire Little America complex, at least for the people who lived there. That and the food.

Orville didn't notice that he had failed to connect the nozzle of the grease gun solidly to the joint under the left rear wheel of the Coupe de Ville, so bemused was he by the sight of his cousin Owen driving a truck. A long rope of grease hung from the bottom of the car and coiled on top of Orville's right shoe, slowing and speeding with each *thump* from the grease machine. He finally released the trigger, dropped the grease gun, and kicked the pedal that lowered the hydraulic lift. The giant black Cadillac oozed gently to the floor, landing with a soft sigh. Orville was already half-way out to greet Owen with sincere enthusiasm.

Owen was no less surprised than Orville to find his cousin working as a grease monkey at a gas station in Little America, Wyoming. 'Well, I'll be damned,' he said in his serious, polite, sincere way. 'Cousin Orville!'

'Yes, indeed, Owen. It certainly is a pleasure to see a familiar face in this out-of-the-way place. What brings you through?'

'Just driving the truck for the company,' Owen answered. 'This is a very special shipment.' Just under the trefoil Owen pointed to the small lettering: HOLLINDAY ENTERPRISES, FISSION DIVISION.

'But I thought you were president of the company now,' Orville said. Apparently the company has diversified since Uncle Wilbur's accident, Orville thought.

'And so I am, so I am,' Owen answered vaguely, his keen brown eyes scanning the maze of service islands, restaurants, overnight accommodations, and the neat rows of parked semis.

'You finished that Caddy yet?' Slim Piggot asked, a thin vein of jealousy running through the basalt of his voice. Orville was encroaching on his territory.

'All done,' said Orville. 'Listen, Owen, why don't you stay the night? It's getting late, and we can go get some dinner, have a drink, talk over old times. How about it?'

As Owen answered him in the affirmative, Orville traced his forefinger around the familiar outlines of the yellow and purple radioactivity trefoil.

27

13

The last time Orville had seen that insignia was when he was working as a law clerk to Judge William 'Wild Bill' Carter, whose brother General Richard 'Dick' Carter was a friend of Uncle Wilbur. 'Wild Bill' had gotten his nickname because even though he was a mousy, balding little runt, he displayed an amazingly vicious temper in the court-room. One night at the weekly country club poker game he had told a story about what he had done to a relatively inoffensive criminal named Ray Creech, whose recent act of antisocial behaviour was organizing his most baroque escape to date from the county jail. The jail was a notoriously easy place to leave; most prisoners simply walked out, but Creech had concocted an insulting plan that included knotted sheets, shoe polish, coffee grounds, fake cell bars made from rolled newspaper, revolvers carved out of soap, etc. The whole thing was an affront to legal dignity.

When he finished the story about what he had done to this dangerous sociopath, the other poker players had laughed so hard they spilled their martinis. Tears rolled down their cheeks, and Andrew Winkler slapped the table at the height of one of his spasms of laughter and said, 'That's wild, Bill.' Everyone called the judge 'Wild Bill' after that.

Creech himself, who always repaired to the Blind Pig Saloon around the corner from the jail and drank beer until he was picked up, had got very drunk the night of this particular escape. His absence wasn't noticed for some hours, which made Creech especially bitter. He was arrested again some years later, at the age of seventy-seven, for selling pornographic comic books on Vine Street. Judge Carter got to try that case as well, and this time he unloaded the entire *Civil and Criminal Code*, all one hundred and twenty-seven pounds of it, on Ray Creech. Almost all the comic books seized in the arrest were locked in Judge Carter's hall closet behind his golf clubs. One, of course, fell into the hands of Patrolman Hiram Quint.

Orville had gone to work for Judge Carter right out of the army because his father wanted him to and Orville had nothing

28

better to do. Yet. He was biding his time. Orville's job was to
assist Wild Bill in drafting legislation that would transfer all
control over fissionable materials to the military, specifically
to the army. Wild Bill's brother Dick had asked him for some
suggestions he could pass along to friendly congressmen.

'Bill,' General Carter had said to him over the phone from
the Pentagon, 'the only way we can restore balance in this
country is to take the big bombs away from the air force and
put them in army hands. After all, the bombs are on the ground
most of the time, and the ground is army territory!' Orville,
who had served his country by servicing those very bombs, had
benefited from that very piece of legislation. Now his job with
Judge Carter was to help make sure that all fissionables were
removed from civilian control, since civilians didn't know what
to do with them, and given to the army, which did.

Orville knew a great deal about the workings of the big
bombs, but he had also learned a lot about the law, and about
security precautions, and about the dangers of an ambitious
military.

'Yes, sir,' he told Judge Carter in a voice ringing with false
outrage, 'we certainly have to get this stuff away from civilians.
They'll just waste it on medicine and stuff like that. After all,
there are enemies everywhere eager to scour democracy from
the face of the world.'

'Good thinking, boy,' said Judge Carter.

Dad would be proud of me, thought Orville. I can lie like a pro.

14

The first time Orville had found it necessary to tell a deliberate
lie was when he was seventeen years old.

He was down in the cellar, a cool if somewhat damp place, in
a small closet where he kept his high school chemistry project.
Orville's indifference to science was based in part on his inability
to add or subtract, but lately he had been spending a lot of time
with this project, and Senior began to hope that Orville might be
preparing himself for a place in the industrial pharmaceuticals
business.

In fact, Orville knew next to nothing about chemistry, but he thought that a little saltpetre, sulphur and charcoal mixed together made a pretty good gunpowder, so he was testing various proportions.

'What the hell are you doing down there, Orville?' his father shouted down the stairs into the gloom of laundry and laboratory.

'Unh, oh, nothing, Dad.'

'Probably jerking off,' Orville heard his father mutter under his breath. Senior had real doubts.

'That's it, Dad,' Orville said. That was his lie. He knew such activities made you crazy, so it seemed appropriate to agree. Senior thought his son was crazy anyway.

It was a lie because Orville was actually constructing a bomb. He tested his latest batch by setting fire to a small pile of it. It fizzed in a satisfactory way, producing a choking cloud of black smoke.

That night he connected his bomb to the distributor of his father's Coupe de Ville. The next morning he waited anxiously at the dining-room window for his father to start the car and disappear in an enormous black cloud.

'Flora,' his father shouted from the recesses of his dressing room. His wife had been named after the Roman goddess of vegetation because she had been conceived one humid summer afternoon in 1925 in her parents' truck garden behind their stately Fourth Street home in Altoona, Pennsylvania, where her father, Harold Beard, did a vast business supplying equipment to the local coal mines. The equipment was reconditioned by *his* father in Uniontown, and was priced slightly higher than the competition, though it was of slightly inferior quality. Mr Beard had a classical turn of mind.

The conception was witnessed by the Beards's neighbour, Miss Walters, whose house was so situated as to provide a clear view between the two rows of sweet corn where the activity was taking place. Miss Walters knew she shouldn't continue to watch the obscene spectacle of Mr Beard's naked buttocks waving and plunging in the irregular pool of sunshine that poured through the leaves of the elm tree, but she seemed to be paralyzed like a frog about to be gigged. Even after Mr Beard had hauled himself off his wife, and the frenzied shaking of her legs, which had been sticking straight up into the air on either side of Mr Beard's bucking bottom, had subsided to a tremor, and the two of them had staggered out of the corn with nothing on below the waist, and had walked with their sticky arms about one another through the screen door to their kitchen, Miss Walters continued to stare at the place where it had all been happening.

For weeks after that she stayed after school and wrote 'I did not see it happen' over and over on the blackboard, but gradually the 'not' dropped from the sentence, and she felt a strange weakness in her thighs.

'I can't find my goddam club tie,' said Mr Hollinday, husband to the goddess of vegetation.

'It's in the laundry, dear,' she answered from the kitchen. Fortunately Orville had removed all traces from yesterday's furtive bomb-making, so he sat with seeming calm in the dining-room, pretending to read.

Finally his father went out to the car, and Orville held his breath.

Nothing happened. After an agonizing amount of time Senior came back into the house. He was fuming. 'The goddam car won't start.' The words sounded like someone chewing gristle.

When the mechanic arrived, he told Mr Hollinday that it looked as though his distributor cap had exploded.

'Goddam car,' said Senior.

15

'Do you like Mexican food?' Orville asked his cousin Owen. The two of them were sitting on the edge of the concrete platform that supplied the foundation for the entire complex of Little America. Under their feet the brown stubble of semi-desert began.

'Sure,' said Owen. His eyes darted around like a pair of caged weasels, desperately looking for something to rest on. Orville had taken him to the north edge of Little America, so Interstate 80 was not visible. The flat, uninteresting ground stretched to the horizon, where it merged with the muddy grey sky. There were no ripples in the ground, no fences dividing fields, no telephone poles marching to the distances, no birds toppling and wheeling in the gathering gloom, no motion of prairie dogs or gophers questing through the stubble. In front of their eyes, nothing happened.

Behind them there was lots of action. The massive neon signs had begun their nightly Darwinian struggle for attention. Half of them advertised various brands of gasoline; the rest offered lodging for the night.

'The extraordinary thing about this place,' said Orville with relish, 'is that there is no real town here whatsoever. This is, quite simply, the largest service station in the world. There are no locals, no natives of the place. Yet. Of course, there soon will be – it's only a matter of time before some of the pregnant girls will want to have their babies at home, or at the clinic here, instead of going all the way to Rock Springs. Then there will be natives.'

As the darkness pooled around them, Orville stared out over the plain and thought for a while about his plan. It seemed good. 'Then this will become a town,' he said, 'and it will be all over. The dream will end. Let's go eat.'

Orville's plan was simple. He was going to introduce Owen to the deaf-mute girl at the Taco House. If dashing old Owen will mess around with a girl like Bobo Winkler, Orville thought, he can certainly mess around with Juanita.

Everyone called the deaf-mute girl Juanita. No one knew her real name, even Harriet Milburn, who owned the Taco House franchise in Little America. Harriet, a stringy shrew in her middle fifties, thought it was important to have a pretense of south-of-the-border atmosphere in her restaurant. That was Juanita.

Orville ordered by holding up four fingers. Two Number 4s. Then, while Owen was glancing around the room, Orville pointed at his cousin and winked at Juanita. A crusty smile spread over her incredible face and she nodded.

When Juanita brought Owen his Number 4, two clam tacos and a cream cheese enchilada, she leaned across him to put down the hot sauce. The front of her peasant blouse fell open, and Owen stared deep into the mysterious depths of her dusky brown bosom. Time was suddenly suspended for him; the long shuddering intake of the aroma of her ripe globes seemed to last forever. Owen's soul was a white wall on which the tiny self of his lust began to write 'I love you' in purple finger paints.

It was done. Owen inhaled in quick nervous breaths the rest of the meal and stared dazedly at Juanita.

'Like me to fix you up?' asked Orville over his dish of green pepper ice-cream.

'Oh, yeah,' said Owen. Small screws at the hinges of his jaw seemed to have come loose. 'That girl is certainly the ugliest girl I've ever seen,' he finished, completely entranced.

16

Owen's wife Margot was the most stunningly beautiful woman anyone had ever seen. When her exquisite even white teeth bit down on a potato chip with a dollop of cheese dip on it, every male in the room swooned with desire. When she tilted her head and gazed into her date's face with her lambent brown eyes, listening to his words, he felt his importance swell to fill the universe. When the silk lining of her camel's-hair coat slid from her perfect creamy shoulders into her escort's waiting hands, the sound it made sent electric spasms of ecstasy choruscating down his spine.

Orville tried every Christmas and every summer through high school, through Harvard and Yale Law and on leave from the army, to get a date with Margot. She always refused him with such a husky warmth in her voice, such a tone of genuine sorrow and regret, that even though she clearly had only the vaguest notion who he was, he felt truly honoured that she had turned him down.

Even Owen, all teeth and Terry and the Pirates jaw as he was, had to pursue her. He courted her with gallantry and concern, with flowers and perfume, with poetry and passion. He became first her escort, then her beau. Finally he got her into a room at the El Rancho Motel on the highway near the factory where his father manufactured a small part for jet engines.

Her dazzling teeth nibbled gently on his earlobes as he pumped his slim but muscular hips solemnly and rhythmically into the gorgeous swell of her groin. Her hands moved gently up and down his spine as he churned and ground as though he were making butter the old-fashioned way, which in a way he was. He moved with gentleness and love, but firmly and tirelessly, using every technique his vast experience had taught him.

Her eyes stared dreamily at the ceiling of Room 114 of the El

Rancho Motel. She heard in the distance the periodic sound of cubes tumbling down in the ice machine outside the door, the romantic swish of traffic passing in the rainy street. She saw on the ceiling vistas of arbors drenched in the perfume of roses, willow trees weeping sadly into the placid waters of lily ponds, herself running in slow motion holding her luscious heaps of petticoats correctly above the ankles as her tiny feet touched lightly on the new-mown grass of her daddy's vast plantation and rose again into the heady scented air. In his study her grey-haired daddy, powerful and kind, was smoking his pipe and running the business of the plantation, and waited for her.

'Oh, Owen,' she murmured into the short hair behind his ear. 'That's wonderful.' She sailed through the humid honey-suckle air. 'Ooooh. Oh. Owen.'

Her legs gave a delicious little shiver and she locked her perfect ankles behind Owen's knees.

Owen, his nose crushed into the sweat-sodden motel pillow, managed to gasp as he came in a long shuddering spasm like the death throes of a slaughtered hog, in a voice strangled in ecstasy, 'Will you marry me?'

'Of course,' said Margot, sitting up with such a sudden twist that Owen's exhausted body flopped off the bed and he beeped his final dwindling drops on to the maroon wall-to-wall carpet of Room 114.

'That's why I slept with you, silly.'

17

Senior Hollinday, six feet one and one half inches tall, was the same height as his nephew Owen, though a bit heavier. They stood side by side at Owen's wedding reception.

'You mean she slept with you in order to marry you?' he asked, incredulous.

'Yes, sir,' said Owen. He didn't look as happy as his relatives expected him to look on his wedding day.

The reception was being held in the entrance hall and upstairs dining-room of the same country club from which, two years before, Owen had slipped away to the eighteenth tee to diddle

Bobo Winkler. It seemed as if the same Christmas holly twined around the fluted columns, although it was now the June after Owen's second year at Harvard Law. His father had not yet made his final inspection of the bomb shelter.

Senior was outraged by Owen's story. He was outraged first because Owen *had* disclosed it to him, and second because he had no idea women still did that sort of thing.

Mainly he was outraged because not ten minutes earlier he had been dancing with the unspeakable radiance and grace of the new bride glowing in his arms, and he had felt a shameful but undeniable twitching in his trousers that had forced him to release Margot to her groom sooner than he would ever have wished, and he couldn't believe that this new object of his every fantasy could be capable of such calculation. And he didn't want to believe she was not a virgin.

Owen's unease increased when at that moment he spotted his cousin Orville manoeuvring Bobo Winkler's hefty torso across the dance floor towards him.

'Ah, Owen,' said Orville, and with a final flourish he twirled Bobo around to face, for the first time since he had loomed over her under his Yale football blanket on the eighteenth tee that clouded December night, the figure of her secret love, before whom her eyes remained bashfully lowered. 'Owen, you remember Bobo Winkler, don't you?' she heard Orville ask.

And Owen's reply, 'Of course I do,' after only a moment's hesitation. 'Bobo, how are you? You certainly are looking, er, fit,' in his deeply sincere way.

A strange flush, or rash, spread over the exposed part of her chest, a flush that her mother might have seen as a pretty blush in response to a compliment, but that Orville, to the delight of the furtive sadist in his brain, saw as a combination of discomfort and disappointment.

There was a long, excruciating silence. Finally Owen bowed to the inevitable and invited Bobo to dance. Orville released her with a gesture of feigned reluctance and raced nonchalantly across the dance floor, as if such a thing were possible, to hurl himself on to the bride, with whom he danced three boxy steps before his father arrived to cut in, his trouser front now falling impeccably straight from belt to inseam.

Senior had smiled as he watched Owen dance off with Bobo Winkler. He knew all about Owen's escapade with her; it was, in fact, common country club knowledge, having been witnessed by no fewer than three employees and seven guests. Senior had frankly never liked Owen much, and since his first dance that night with Margot he detested him. He knew his wife Flora liked Owen, however, so he kept his own counsel.

As soon as he had sent Orville packing and once more held Margot in his arms, his malicious smile faded and a dreamy film covered his eyes. He noticed that the bridal gown was firm and filled with ample petticoats, so what the hell, he thought, as the natural tide began to flood his pecker. What the hell.

18

What the hell, thought Owen, hesitating for a moment before following Juanita into her tiny Airstream trailer. Owen always said What the hell to himself at moments like this. Afterwards he always said That was terrific.

The door slammed behind him with a disconcerting sound of finality, and he turned back briefly in panic. When he turned around again, Juanita pushed him down on the vinyl-covered bench running along one side of the trailer and began to undo his pants. Jesus, thought Owen, his eyes rolling towards the ceiling. Jesus.

Juanita was pulling his J. Press slacks over his shoes with an expert flick of her wrists. Jesus. She carefully unrolled his paisley Jockey shorts down his smooth, muscular legs. Owen sat there, feeling very peculiar, in his Arrow shirt and black, well-polished Wellington boots, his highly trained prick twitching at half-mast, as though uncertain in this situation which way to go.

Then she pulled her peasant blouse over her head, and the enormous dusky globes that had first entranced him bounded into view. She may have had a face to send a truck driver tight-lipped from the room, but for large, oblate spheroids of earth-shaped breasts Owen, for one, had never seen the like. A thin silvery trickle of drool leaked from the corner of Owen's perfectly chiselled mouth, as though he were a water bed with a tiny puncture.

Juanita let her skirt drop to the floor and revealed an even more bounteous, more generous behind than Owen thought possible. And then, in absolute silence, she floated towards him under the harsh fluorescents of the trailer and slowly, oh Jesus, enveloped his entire body like a gigantic rubber cloud.

Outside, the huge diesels backed and whined, air brakes hissed and squealed, the clatter of plates and conversation from Young Foo's Chow Mein Palace wafted across the parking plaza, the myriad of neon signs hummed and crackled their beguilements, the bedsprings of dozens of the sixteen hundred motel rooms creaked and bounced in unison, the stars shone crisply on Little America. Inside the Airstream there was perfect silence, perfect pleasure, perfect bliss. Owen thought he might be falling in love, and forgot all about his late dad, his business, his wife, his truck and his cargo.

Orville, of course, had not forgotten. By the time Juanita had engulfed Owen's quivering dingle in her gelid treasure trove, Orville was deftly unlocking the doors to Owen's truck. By the time Juanita had Owen down on the floor, his face buried deep in her pendulous globes, and was churning her enormous bottom around his crackling joystick, Orville was removing four lead containers marked U-235 from the back of the Hollinday Enterprises, Fission Division truck. And by the time Owen's eyes had rolled completely into his skull, leaving only two huge glistening catatonic whites showing, and he had begun to pop his business into the turmoil of Juanita's insides, Orville was carefully reclosing the doors to Owen's diesel.

Suddenly, just as Owen's eyes were beginning to wind downwards once more from the tops of his eye sockets and the iron stiffness of his body to soften, the door of the Airstream crashed open.

'Son of a bitch,' screamed Slim Piggot from the open door, vibrating like a marionette controlled by a palsied operator.

'Son of a bitch.'

19

Senior Hollinday might have found his wife with Andrew had he taken the usual way down the stairs to the men's room next to the Walnut Bar at the country club.

The Walnut Bar had gotten its name because someone on the Faculties Committee thought it would be nice if the tables had, instead of imitation wooden bowls filled with potato chips and popcorn, imitation wooden bowls filled with walnuts; this would give, it was felt, a bit more class to an already classy room. In addition, each table had two nutcrackers. There were usually eight or ten regular walnut addicts in the room at any one time, and the din was terrible.

Senior did not go downstairs the usual way because he was attempting to steal after Margot as she glided down the hall to the upstairs ladies' room. She was going, she said, 'to straighten her wedding corsage,' prior to departing with her new groom on their honeymoon trip (the South of France). Senior had followed in hopes of trapping her alone in a deserted corridor.

He realized he would be hard put to explain his presence in this particular hallway should anyone question him, so while half his mind was bent on carefully placing his formal wing tips into the imaginary glass slippers left by Margot's shapely feet on the royal blue carpet, the other half was applied to thinking up some reason to be there.

Just as the heavy pink door sighed shut behind Margot's callipygous dorsum, a busboy from the dining-room entered the hallway from the left. To throw him off the scent, Senior pretended to be lost and asked him where the men's room was.

'Just down these stairs, sir,' said the busboy, pointing back down the way he had come.

If Senior had been going down the main stairs, then, instead of the employee's stairs, he would have heard, from the deep darkness of the downstairs dining-room, the voice of his friend and best customer, Andrew Winkler, saying, 'Son of a bitch. Oh, son of a bitch.'

And later, had he not been in the men's room splashing cold water on his face and attempting to control his tortured breathing, he might have peered into the room to see what could have been agitating his friend.

He would have seen Andrew in the darkest corner at the far end of the dining-room, backed against the wall next to an artificial palm tree. And he would have seen Flora Hollinday pressing her still-luscious form against the owner of one hundred and thirty-six Kernel Korn's Drive-In restaurants throughout the Midwest.

Then, as his eyes adjusted to the gloom shrouding the polished

38

wood tables and stacked chairs, he might have seen the vertical mouth of Andrew Winkler's formal trousers' open fly deeply engaged in the delicious process of devouring Flora's right arm half-way to the elbow. It might even have seemed as though the mouth were gagging a bit on the arm, so strangled and contorted was the activity inside.

Had Senior then crept a bit closer, however, he might have heard his wife's short little gasps of what was clearly not pain, but pleasure and excitement, and he might have noted from the tone of Andrew's voice as he said, 'Son of a bitch. Oh, son of a bitch,' over and over, that he, too, was in no pain.

But if he had got that close Andrew might have seen him, and then there would have been a scene.

Fortunately for everyone, by the time Senior emerged from the men's room with every hair in place and an unruffled smile on his face, Flora and Andrew were back upstairs mixing well with the other guests, and no one at Owen and Margot Hollinday's wedding reception was any the wiser.

Only Andrew was carrying around in his trouser pocket the sweet and sticky secret of what had gone on in the downstairs dining-room.

20

But there was one witness to the rendezvous in the downstairs dining-room. Sergeant Elmo Laurel, twelve-year veteran of the US Army, was on leave visiting his brother Edward, a chef at the country club. Sergeant Laurel's parents had given all their children names beginning with *E* so they would have the same initials – Elmo, Edward, Elizabeth, Eric, Erwin and Etta, whose birth so exhausted Mrs Laurel that she went into a decline from which she never recovered. This had its benefits since Mr Laurel, a man of limited imagination, had been hard-pressed to come up with Etta.

Sergeant Laurel, a cook like his brother, had been watching Edward prepare a béchamel sauce, but he became so impatient with the complex and tiresome way his brother slowly melted the butter, stirred in the sifted flour, poured the boiling salt and milk into the *roux*, and beat the mixture with his stainless steel wire whip, taking care to remove all bits of *roux* from the edges of the pan, and then seasoned the mixture, that he wandered off to explore the interior of the country club. He had never seen this kind of celebration before, where swell folks danced sedately to outdated music.

The army had taught Sergeant Laurel how to make a béchamel sauce completely different from Edward's, in a more simple and streamlined way, practically speaking, that was identical to the way he also prepared *sauce Robert, béarnaise, bercy, bigarde, hollandaise, chaud-froid blanche neige, diable, à l'estragon, trainiera, villeroi, mornay, piquante, mousseline, bâtarde, rémoulade, thermidor, velouté, rouille* and *Grand Marnier*. Nonetheless, Sergeant Laurel thought of himself as an artist with food, not haute cuisine perhaps, no snobbery; but each of his massive creations, he felt, was a work of art. When he prepared his chipped beef on toast, for example, he thought of it not, as those throughout the vast network of American military and paramilitary organizations who had to eat this concoction did, as shit on a shingle, but rather as an extension of his personality, which, in a way, it was. So it pained him somewhat to see his brother ruin a good sauce like that.

Elmo wandered through the phantasmagoric maze of the employees' section of the country club, his attention mildly attracted now by the furnace room, now by the janitor's closets, by the warren of basement kitchens set up to service the downstairs dining-room, by the arrangement of dumbwaiters to send prepared foods and ingredients from one kitchen to the other. He had just cracked open the swinging door to the downstairs dining-room to take a peek at the elegant side of the country club's facilities when he heard a voice in the darkness, saying, 'Son of a bitch, son of a bitch,' over and over. He let the door close gently and peered through the triangular glass window. Just across the dining-room he saw Andrew Winkler and Flora Hollinday. His position afforded him a view of the placement of Mr Winkler's hands, one of which was bent awkwardly into the front of Mrs Hollinday's strapless evening dress, the other of which was clutching spasmodically at her groin.

'Oh, Andrew,' he heard her saying, her breath ragged as she tirelessly milked inside Mr Winkler's fly. 'Talk dirty! Oh, yes, talk dirty!'

'Son of a bitch, oh, son of a bitch,' said Mr Winkler.

Elmo watched until it was over, then rushed upstairs to tell his brother Edward about the hilarious incident in the downstairs dining-room.

21

Orville never got to eat the poached eggs his mother was preparing for him the afternoon following Bobo Winkler's coming-out party. Just as she was buttering the toast, the phone rang.

Oh, boy, thought Orville, this is it! The fact was that Orville had spent two hours in the early morning, between three-thirty and five-thirty, underneath his father's Coupe de Ville, carefully draining the brake fluid from the left-hand side, and all morning he had been lying in bed in an agony of suspense waiting for the phone to ring with the news of the fatal accident.

Flora breathed 'Hello' into the phone and was almost knocked over by the force of Senior's voice. 'Send the little creep down to the office to pick me up,' he shouted through twenty-seven miles of copper wire, switching mechanisms and transfer points into Flora's ear even before the long vowel at the end of 'Hello' had died away. 'I was just getting ready to go out to lunch and the goddam car fritzed out on me again. Goddam car,' he muttered, and hung up with a slam.

'Your father would like you to pick him up at the office, dear,' Mrs Hollinday told her son in tones as sweet and round as a pear falling ripe into his waiting hand. 'Something seems to have gone wrong with the car.'

Uh-oh, thought Orville with a mingled sense of defeat and foreboding. He drove as slowly as possible through the light early afternoon traffic to the HIP Inc. building at the Warren G. Harding Industrial Park. Uh-oh.

When he manoeuvred the family 1963 Ford Ranch Wagon into the executive parking lot, he saw the results of his two hours' work. The dark maroon Coupe de Ville was backed deeply into the rear quarter-panel of a Kernel Korn's Drive-In Restaurant delivery truck that Mr Winkler had driven over to HIP Inc. and parked in the executive parking lot. He and Senior had been on their way to lunch to discuss some business matters, some-

41

thing to do with Mr Winkler's Fritterburgers, perhaps. From the degree of damage, Orville could guess that his father had been in a bad mood when he backed out the car. Some trouble with the Special Sauce, no doubt, Orville mused.

Two mechanics and a tow truck were working on the mess. As Orville walked to his father's office after carefully parking the Ranch Wagon, one of the mechanics followed him in.

Senior and Mr Winkler were sitting on the leather couch in Senior's office, two large drinks on the coffee table in front of them. The huge crystal decanter stood to hand. Senior had given Miss Freemont the afternoon off since it was Christmas Eve.

'You only got about half your brake fluid,' the mechanic told Senior. 'Maybe your brakes don't work too good?'

'Goddam car,' said Orville's father. 'Don't know why I keep buying Cadillacs. They keep going wrong on me.'

His mood seemed to have picked up with the Scotch and water he was drinking. He seemed almost jovial. 'Orville, come on and pour yourself a drink. Did you have a good time at the party last night?'

He winked at Andrew Winkler and took a large Christmas pull on his drink.

22

At first it didn't register on Owen that he was under attack, but gradually the presence of Slim Piggot's ire penetrated Owen's sex-fogged brain. His eyes came into focus, swivelled, and locked on to Slim like two servo-linked radar dishes fixing on a flight of incoming ICBMs.

He began to squirm like an uncontrolled fire hose, but Juanita's buttery buttocks seemed to have melted down either side of his hips and solidified there, effectively pinning him to the floor. Juanita, of course, heard nothing; her back was to the door, and she didn't notice the direction and fixation of Owen's eyes. Indeed, she interpreted his writhing as an indication of renewed interest in intercourse, and she responded with a broad, hideous smile.

Slim danced jerkily into the room, still shouting, 'Son of a

42

bitch. Goddam son of a bitch.' His fist tightly clenched, he swung with all his power at Juanita's head.

She picked that exact time to bend down, still oblivious to Slim's presence, and plant one of her repulsive kisses on Owen's curiously working lips. Slim's fist and powerful arm sailed through the place vacated by Juanita's head and hurtled with all their force into the compact, built-in, concealed refrigerator in the Airstream trailer.

Four things gave way at once: the knuckles of Slim's index, middle and ring fingers collapsed under the impact, and his trick football elbow folded and bent his arm back strangely about three inches out of true in the wrong direction.

Juanita knew nothing of these new developments. Her wondrous, gelid mass, brown as the dusty streets of Nuevo Laredo, quivered with the churning of Owen's frantic, powerful hips, unaware that what motivated them now was fear and not desire.

Nor did she hear Slim's forehead follow his fist and elbow into the tiny refrigerator, so mightily had he swung. The three loud cracks – fist, elbow and forehead – were followed by the soft sighing sound of his body slumping almost in slow motion to the floor.

Very slowly Owen relaxed. Slim seemed to be completely unconscious. Owen's eyes regained a relatively normal appearance. He stopped squirming.

Juanita, in despair that Owen seemed to be losing interest, began a rhythmic clenching and unclenching of some muscles somewhere inside her wonderful interior, and though Owen had an irresistible urge to flee, he found himself drawn once more into the amazing vortex of Juanita's seething Venus's-flytrap. Slim remained motionless; someone had cut all the strings, and he had fallen in a tired heap, his head cradled gently against Owen's right Wellington boot.

'Son of a bitch,' said Owen afterwards. 'That was terrific.'

23

Orville was just beginning to develop a lifelong interest in the potty the day the medium-sized city of Hiroshima was melted down to a large, fused lump of concrete, glass, flesh and hair with the aid of the newly discovered fission process. The bomb was called Big Boy, an ancestor of Big Daddy: thus proving that the child is indeed father to the man. Orville, always a sensitive child, might have been depressed by the news had he been a few years older.

His father was not in the least depressed, however. Lieutenant (JG) Orville Hollinday, Senior, USN, greeted the news, which came to him from the new Philco table model radio in his office, with extraordinary enthusiasm. 'Goddam,' he said to his wife when he got home. 'That'll show those little yellow fascist bastards what we can do!' Lieutenant (JG) Hollinday had a job in Alamanda, California, which he told all his friends, including his wife, was top secret, but which in fact mostly dealt with the logistics of food for navy officers' clubs on the West Coast. The knowledge of standardized foods he picked up in the navy stood him in good stead later, when he founded HIP Inc.'s world-wide empire.

'Yes, dear,' Flora answered him, a bit distracted by her effort to keep Orville's squirming naked form on the training potty she had recently bought.

'Can't that little piece of shit use that thing yet?' Senior asked peevishly, annoyed that his wife wasn't really paying attention to him.

Lurking just under the surface in the turbid shallows of Senior's mind, two conflicting feelings were browsing on the underside of his awareness. First the pride of Alexander after the conquest of Scythia that he had sired a son. He spent the day of Orville's birth making the rounds of Logistics to hand out enormous Cuban cigars to his fellow officers, saying over and over, 'It's a boy. Orville Junior. A boy.'

Floating dully alongside that feeling was an enormous sullen resentment. He never, through Truman and Eisenhower and Kennedy and Johnson and Nixon and Ford and Carter, forgave his wife for having a puny distraction of a child, particularly one who, that second day at the hospital, had peed straight into Senior's face just after Senior had noticed that his son's genitals were abnormally large. This last perception never quite broke the surface, but somewhere inside him Senior felt a sharp pain *ping*. Senior thought it was indigestion and never ate oysters Rockefeller again.

Even when he had dandled his baby boy on his knee, an

44

ecstatic smile smeared across his benign, sallow face, he had referred to Orville as 'that little shit'. Then, Senior genuinely meant this as a term of endearment, a little rib-tickling kidding among buddies, and was gratified when Orville responded with a giggle and a drool. But when Orville spit up on his uniform, Senior would instantly lateral the tiny body to his wife and rush to the kitchen, where he vigorously applied a damp washcloth to his soiled shoulder.

The day the first atomic bomb publicly lifted its fungoid head into the view of an amazed world, Senior pretended to have known about the bomb all along; he was, after all, an important person in the military hierarchy, privy to secrets.

'This'll change the world,' he told his wife. 'Nothing can stop us now. America is the greatest country in the world!'

At that exact moment, Orville produced into the new training potty his first really successful bowel movement.

24

It took Orville several months after he arrived at Little America to get a date with Bobalou Trbochet. Their shifts overlapped, since she worked from 5 a.m. to noon, and he worked from eight until five, but he was put in charge of the lube rack and she worked the gas pumps, so they seemed to belong to different worlds. Nonetheless, Orville secretly watched the Li'l Injun insignia ride smoothly around the station over Bobalou's left breast, and at night he had psycholagnic dreams about Bobalou's plump lips.

In the end it was Bobalou who asked him out.

'Orville,' she said to him one glowering Wyoming noon late in the fall of 1974, 'why don't you and me go for a ride in my brand-new nineteen seventy-four Dodge van?' Bobalou was a very direct girl who believed in speaking her mind. 'You're a nice-looking boy, nice wavy hair, terrific green eyes, you've got a nice build and you always talk polite. I know you've been watching me when I go out to the pumps, but I don't think you know that I've been watching you too. I like the way your hands move when you do a lube job. But especially there's something about you, something intense and serious and mysterious, a kind of glow. I don't know. Something.'

Bobalou had never before spoken to Orville at such length, and he was completely stunned; it was as though his every *Playboy* fantasy had suddenly leaped from the centrefold of his imagination into moist pulsating actual life and led him by the hand into the warm confines of a mirrored bachelor pad with five thousand dollars' worth of stereo equipment and a round water bed with black satin sheets. Not since his strangely adventurous evening with Mary Lou Perkins had he felt such a powerful sense of heightened perception, and *that* evening he had been motivated by his terrible rage at his father and hadn't really noticed Mary Lou.

This was different. He forgot his father. Chuckie Chipwood was over at Young Foo's Chow Mein Palace listening to the Warriors-Pistons game on the radio and eating lunch. Slim Piggot was at the General Motors dealer in Rock Springs picking up a new water pump for a lavender 1972 Chevrolet Impala with 57,396 miles on it, and there was nothing for Orville to do but stare stupidly at Bobalou's promising mouth. The grey November sky, which seemed to be pregnant with the season's first snowfall, suddenly took on an eerie luminescence and the Li'l Injun station pulsated with every heartbeat.

'OK' was all he could manage to say.

'I'll pick you up at five,' said Bobalou, and she sashayed out across the concrete apron of Little America with such grace and bounty towards the Crossroads Drive-In that Orville watched long after she had disappeared from sight, and then he sat and stared at the lavender Impala, which belonged to a liquor salesman from Des Moines, a kind man who still wore two-tone shoes and loved his family – his wife, Sally, his three children (two boys and a girl) and his dog. In the two and a half days he had been grounded in Little America waiting for his car to be fixed, he had eaten in seven different drive-in restaurants and the Coffee Shoppe, and had watched seventeen hours of television in his motel room.

Orville didn't notice when it began with great solemnity to snow big soft flakes into the sudden hush of Little America.

25

It was snowing the night Orville planted the dynamite inside each of the four wheels of his father's new royal blue 1965 Cadillac Coupe de Ville. It was a damp, annoying, dense snow, filled with particulate industrial waste, and it fell from an invisible sky with an oppressive meanness on most of the Midwest. It had dumped four and seventeen one-hundredths inches of slick, hazardous snow on the city in two hours, and it showed no signs of letting up. Orville thought it was wonderful.

He had tiptoed down the back stairs at three in the morning with his stolen dynamite and his home-made timing device and had discovered the snow when he looked out the back door. It fell in nicely with his plan.

Senior always drove twelve and seven-tenths miles from his home to his office. At exactly ten miles from home he would be driving down a curving stretch of the Louisa May Alcott Freeway towards the Warren G. Harding Industrial Park. The hill and the incline would be enough, thought Orville, as he gazed out at the layer of snow on the driveway, snow that seemed to ripple with malevolence. But this snow should certainly clinch the deal.

Orville connected the timer to the odometer of the Cadillac, set the dynamite to go off in exactly ten miles, and softly stole back into the house.

Senior was in the kitchen in a blaze of fluorescent light, a bluish, humming light that glinted off the chrome and white ceramic fixtures and dazzled Orville when he came in from the semi-gloom of the garage. Senior was preparing a sandwich. A loaf of Wonder Bread, that built healthy bodies at least eight ways, and possibly twelve, sat on the counter. One slice had already been spread with a thick layer of cottage cheese and dill pickle. Senior was in the process of slicing some pepperoni into very thin pieces when Orville came into the kitchen.

'Hello, son,' said Senior kindly. His spectacles, which he only needed when he wanted to see things closer than two feet away, were pushed up on top of his head. He smiled distractedly at

47

Orville, carefully sliced one more piece off the pepperoni, and put the knife down.

Orville stood rooted to the floor. He felt as though a vicious cold front had just passed through his torso leaving hundreds of people dead from exposure in its wake.

'I was just out. Looking at the snow. It's snowing.' I hope he doesn't go out to look for tracks. I hope he doesn't notice my shoes aren't wet. I hope he goes to bed. I hope he eats his sandwich. I hope he's half asleep. Orville's mind spun like wheels in a snowbank. I hope he doesn't get stuck in the driveway tomorrow. Oh. My. God.

Senior ate his sandwich and went to bed. 'Good night, son,' he said warmly as he went back up the stairs, leaving Orville standing in an imaginary pool of melted snow.

The next morning Senior called his wife for the third time in as many years.

'Do you know what happened to that goddam car of mine? A brand-new goddam Cadillac Coupe de Ville? Do you?' he asked her over the phone.

'All four hubcaps suddenly flew off in the middle of the Louisa May Alcott Freeway. That's what happened!

'Goddam car.'

26

Senior was a mild, kind man who walked around in a barely controlled rage most of the time. He honestly felt that he was benign and friendly and that he could take care of anything and anybody. He was a great admirer of Will Rogers, and he was fond of saying that he had never met a man he didn't like. He thought he even liked Orville, though he knew he'd never amount to a hill of beans.

Lieutenant Orville Hollinday, Senior, USN (Ret.), left the Navy in 1949 and spent a year travelling around the Midwest looking for opportunity. In 1950 he found it, and he hired a lawyer to incorporate for him.

'I never met a man I didn't like,' he told his lawyer, Bill Carter, who would later become a judge and would be nicknamed

'Wild Bill'. 'Will Rogers always said that, and those are good words to live by. Everyone in the world has his use, even a Russian.' That's what Senior meant when he quoted Will Rogers: he never met a man he couldn't use.

'True. How true,' Bill Carter said.

They were sitting in Bill's oak-panelled corner office in the Carter Building. The office looked out on a small park in which daffodils and tulips were just beginning to open up to the early spring sun. The window facing the park was open, and the damp, fervid smells of the season wafted in. Fortunately the building was far enough removed so they didn't have to smell the river.

'But why?' Bill asked, leaning back in his leather chair. 'Why industrial pharmaceuticals? What are industrial pharmaceuticals?'

'I'm not really sure at the moment,' Senior answered. He carefully peeled the wrapper from a fresh Cuban cigar, snipped off the end with a silver tool he took from his pocket, and lit it, filling the air around his head with a thick, obscuring, aromatic smoke that completely smothered the odour of daffodils and tulips.

'I'm not sure,' he repeated, shaking out his match. 'But it will be the coming thing. For example: the war in Korea. There will be a demand for drugs in bulk. It will take some time to gear up for that, of course, and I plan to be there. In the meantime, though, and over the long haul, I plan to manufacture a Special Sauce.'

Bill was fascinated. 'A Special Sauce?' he urged.

'Oh. Yes. Sorry.' Senior had drifted off for a moment. He offered Bill a cigar. Though Bill was not old at the time, he already had the peculiar rabbity eyes nested in absolutely circular pools of wrinkles that characterized his later years, when Orville worked for him as a clerk.

'A Special Sauce for fastfoods.' Senior said it as one word, 'fastfoods'. 'Fastfoods are the coming thing.'

Bill smiled. Although his teeth were green, his breath, oddly enough, was not too bad. He was thinking about the fortune to be made in fast foods.

'Yes,' said Senior, looking upwards into the swirling ribbons of pungent cigar smoke that coiled over his head. 'Definitely the coming thing!'

27

There were a lot of things Orville didn't know about life the first time his father drove him across the country to Camp Tomahawk, a lovely spot on a lovely lake in the lovely mountains of Idaho with lovely rustic log cabins and T-shirts with CAMP TOMAHAWK printed on them over the camp insignia – a large stylized tomahawk with vaguely abstract feathers stuck to the handle and inky blood dripping from the blade. The camp was designed to instill manly virtues in the little campers, aged eight to fifteen, and Orville's father felt that his son needed some manly virtues instilled. Orville wasn't particularly fond of sports, and Senior worried he would turn out something near to trash because of it.

Orville was nine years old. He sat far over near the door of his father's 1953 Cadillac Couple de Ville and stared out at the passing June countryside. These were, his father told him, the Great Plains. Orville believed it.

His mother, who at this time still believed that a lifetime of service to her husband, whom she had married rather young, was the noblest existence to which a woman could dedicate herself, had spent several days sewing name tags into Orville's underwear.

'Why do I have to go away to camp?' Orville sat at her feet on the floor with a large, crudely fashioned HIP Inc. toy delivery truck. 'Vroom, vroom,' he said under his breath as he rolled the truck back and forth on its wooden wheels.

'Oh, Orville, it will be so wonderful. Fresh mountain air, canoeing, camping out in the woods, lots of kids your age. I'm sure you'll have a wonderful time.'

Orville agreed that if his mother said it would be wonderful, why, then, it probably would be wonderful, though he felt uneasy about all the other kids, the camping out, the canoeing and sports. Especially the sports.

Every couple of months his father would take him out in the backyard for a game of catch. He'd throw a soft ball at him as hard as he could for a minute or two and then stomp back into

50

the house in disgust and say to his wife, 'That little shit can't even catch a ball!' Orville's confidence never developed any real strength after these sessions.

Now he sat on the slick brown leather upholstery of his father's vast automobile and stared out at the distant mountains. They had already crossed the mighty Mississippi, a landmark of such awesome significance to his father that Orville learned how to spell it, to be rewarded by Senior by the anointing of a few oily drops of praise on his tousled head.

They passed through towns, hundreds of towns, towns that Orville was sure were full of cowboys and possibly Indians. He saw general stores with post offices in them; he saw grain elevators; he saw tidy white farmhouses in the middle of vast emptiness surrounded by stands of slender trees and fields enclosed with barbed-wire fences; he saw car dealerships and miles of automobile graveyards.

But most of all, suddenly, auspiciously, as though the Phantom had conjured it out of nowhere, he saw rising up around him the magic splendour of Little America.

They had stopped there for gas. At that time, in 1953, it had nothing of the glory it would later achieve: only twenty-five pumps, the old-fashioned kind with round glass tops that enclosed little red balls dancing around on top of the gasoline, and only two places to eat, but to Orville it offered a more powerful magic than anything Walt Disney could produce. They ate a meal in the small coffee shop, a real hamburger prepared by hand in front of them by a friendly but sloppy cook with the most enormous stomach Orville had ever seen.

Senior never even remembered the name of the place.

28

One thing Senior did remember was his newly acquired niece by marriage, Margot. He would sit at his desk at HIP Inc. manfully trying to plot the destruction of yet another competitor and suddenly begin shaking all over just under the skin. He tried stiff Scotch from the crystal decanter. He tried pacing his office patio. He tried gazing at the smokestacks of the HIP factory across the Warren G. Harding Industrial Park. He tried cold showers in his birch-panelled office bathroom. He tried golf.

'Fore!' he shouted, and swung viciously at the ball, which had been sitting smugly on a red plastic tee. Wild Bill was unable to conceal his green smirk of satisfaction as the ball sliced nastily into the rough on the fourteenth fairway. Senior's game was off, and Judge Carter figured to himself that that may be one of the few days he might actually win a few dollars off his client. Senior had already topped ninety and still had five holes to go.

'Goddammit.' Senior sounded as though his mouth were on backwards and he was speaking down his own trachea to someone hiding in his lungs. His face had begun to clot up on the seventh green, where he four-putted, and by now it was so dark that it looked as though it might be able to destroy several small towns in Kansas in a matter of minutes. Wild Bill was delighted.

Senior paid him off in the locker-room, and after an extended cold shower they retired to the Walnut Room for drinks. As soon as they were seated Wild Bill began attacking walnuts with an enthusiasm that did nothing to conceal the buoyancy of triumph. This would have annoyed Senior further had he not already been so distracted.

After his second drink he shook himself out of it. 'Bill,' he said suddenly. 'I need a little legal advice. As you know I've been manufacturing the Special Sauce for several years now, and it's been by far the most successful of our enterprises . . .'

Judge Carter nodded; his share had repaid him handsomely over the years.

Senior frowned at his drink. 'I've heard,' he continued, 'that there will be an investigation, some testing of random samples taken from around the country and so on, of the Special Sauce. You know the sort of meddling the feds are always doing. Well, what I'm saying is, you know what would happen if . . .'

'If the FDA really looks closely at the Special Sauce. Yes, indeed.' Wild Bill now looked very serious himself, his dry reptilian lips pursed quirkily over his green teeth. He dropped his nutcracker on the heap of walnut shells and emitted a long raspy whistle. 'Not only might profits be damaged. There could be very serious consequences.' Bill paused for a long moment. 'Let me think about it. I may be able to do something.'

'I wish you'd do that, Bill. And on top of that, I also wish you'd . . .'

Judge Carter never learned what else Senior wanted him to do. At that moment Margot walked into the room wearing a tight pair of electric red shorts and a halter top, and Senior made the most peculiar wheezing sounds that caused everyone in the room to rush to his assistance, including the bartender, but excluding Margot, who walked right through the room and out the opposite door without noticing a thing.

29

When Slim recovered consciousness he found himself staring up into the incredible face of his beloved Juanita, whose lop-sided toothy grin showered him with radiance and love and whose soft, sloppy hands engulfed his left hand like a carnivorous plant closing over a fly.

Slim had no idea who she was.

He stared past her head at the ceiling, which was as blank and white as his mind. His eyes moved slowly along the bottom edge of the enormous bandage covering his head to the eye-brows; he sensed that he was lying on a hospital bed. On the other side of the bed, opposite Juanita, sat his boss and friend, Chuckie Chipwood, with his Sony transistor radio in his lap. From the tiny earphone plugged into Chuckie's left ear came the tinny sounds of a crowd going wild.

'Third period and the score's tied eighty-seven to eighty-seven. What happened, ole buddy?' Chuckie asked when he noticed Slim looking at him. He didn't remove the earphone.

'Huh?'

'I said, "What happened?" Damn, the Celtics just got a basket. You got a busted hand, your elbow is all bent out of shape, you got a concussion – looks like you got hit by a truck or something. Didja get in a fight?'

'Huh?'

'What happened to him?' Chuckie asked Juanita, giving up on Slim. At eight-thirty that morning Juanita had wheeled Slim into the Little America Medical Clinic behind the Coffee Shoppe in a wheelbarrow she had borrowed from the Standard station next door to her Airstream trailer. She had stayed by his side, though naturally she had been stolidly silent.

She remained silent when Chuckie asked her what had happened. He didn't expect an answer anyway; he was just making conversation until Slim recovered his wits.

The two of them sat on either side of the starched, antiseptic bier, while Slim Piggot lay staring at the ceiling for another hour. But for the small sounds of the game progressing towards the end of the final period in Chuckie's earphone, the room was entirely silent. The silence seemed to be settling like sediment around them, slowly, layer after layer, creating a thick stratum of solid rock that filled the room, encasing them like fossils. No one moved.

Slim's eyes fixed on the speck of a bluebottle fly that hung upside down from the ceiling, washing its feet with quick, pedantic gestures. Finally the fly walked primly across the ceiling towards the window, but Slim's eyes remained fixed in place, not bothering to follow it. Then, faintly, through the cinder-block walls of the clinic, the musical rumble of traffic on Interstate 80 hummed through the room, lulling its occupants like the eternal background rhythms of the tides in the vast, maternal sea.

The game on Chuckie's Sony ended, and Howard Cosell interviewed the manager of the losing team, but Chuckie didn't listen. He had fallen asleep.

Suddenly the door banged open and Orville bustled into the room, an enormous paper flower from the Gifte Shoppe, which was attached to the Coffee Shoppe, in his hand. 'Wow,' he said, 'I just heard the news. What happened to Slim?'

Orville of course knew perfectly well what had happened to Slim. His cousin Owen, who had finally collapsed into his bunk behind the driver's seat in the diesel rig and dreamed of huge thighs glistening wetly, met Orville in the morning at the Li'l Injun station where Orville was working alone, and told him everything, not quite sure whether to laugh or cry.

'But Jesus,' Owen added, 'it was terrific!'

30

'I'm selling a book called *The Jesus Connection*,' announced the bearded individual sitting next to Orville in the almost deserted Coffee Shoppe one afternoon in the early summer of 1976. 'But actually, it's a cover.' He chuckled. 'Got it? A cover. Cover; book?' The voice sounded a bit familiar to Orville. The bad joke also sounded familiar.

'It gives me an excuse to travel around. Meet people. Ask a few questions.' The bearded individual had arrived in Little America twenty minutes before driving a 1968 Volkswagen Beetle, light tan, with mud-splattered Indiana licence plates. The Beetle had 136,000 thousand miles on it.

The waitress was standing by the cash register picking her teeth with a mint-flavoured toothpick.

'I'd like an egg salad sandwich,' the bearded individual told her. 'Actually,' he said, turning to Orville, 'I'm a secret agent.'

'Gaaa. Eggs!' shouted Orville, the tumblers of memory triggered by the order. 'I didn't recognize you with the beard. How the hell are you?' Orville hadn't seen him since the army. 'It's been six, seven years?'

'Knew you right away, Orville,' Eggs Freebnik said with a grin. 'Came looking for you, in fact, here in Little America. It looks like your dream is coming true, eh? Do you have your own gas pump yet?'

'Sure do. I'm even a partner in the Li'l Injun gas station here with a guy named Chuckie Chipwood, a fellow from Billings, Montana. I man the pumps, do an occasional lube job, give orders to my girl-friend, Bobalou Trbochet, and the hired man, a guy named Slim Piggot who lost his memory in an interesting way, I'll tell you about it sometime, they both work at the Li'l Injun station. But tell me about yourself, what do you mean you're a secret agent?' Orville was having trouble controlling himself; he and Eggs had had some great times in the army.

'Well, I'm not *really* a secret agent, you know, but I get to go around in disguise like this to check up on security arrangements for the transportation of nuclear materials in this country.

Sort of an incognito uranium marshal, you know, for the government. I just watch trucks, see how they're locked, what precautions private companies take, whether anyone could be stealing fissionables, that sort of thing.

'Also find out how it moves around. Like here, for instance. A number of trucks carry stuff through Little America. You notice them coming through, how often they stop, how long, that sort of thing?'

'I see them coming through on occasion,' said Orville. He peered into his coffee cup as though he might have lost something in there. 'Gives me a kind of nostalgic feeling about the old days in the army, you know. Remember the Bomb Room?' Orville changed the subject.

Eggs certainly did remember the Bomb Room. 'Yeah. Big Momma, Big Daddy, and Wee Wee.' Orville blushed slightly at the mention of Big Daddy, but he was smiling.

'By the way,' Eggs said, pausing for a moment as the waitress dropped his egg salad sandwich in front of him. 'Did you ever kill your father?'

'Naw,' said Orville. 'That all seems a long time ago.'

31

Oh God, Senior Hollinday thought, slumped into his hardwood chair amid the hazy richwood smells and walnut crunch of the country club bar, unaware of his wheezing, of the slaps of the bartender or of the murmured concerns of Wild Bill Carter about golf or the impending FDA investigation of the Special Sauce. He was thinking one thing: Oh God, I hunger up her long legs, I hunger I want to put my lips my mouth around her foot, the foot that springs so wonderfully about the tennis court to swallow her foot and eat my way up her smooth slender ankle her delicate bones and the amazing swell of her calf so smooth the fine small bones of her knee the small bobbing of the flat round kneebone as she walks the way it flexed under her wedding gown oh God when I danced with her at the reception and the incredible hard-on I got to eat oh God the smooth firm skin of her thigh and then oh my God what's under there dark moist Jesus I think I'm coming.

And that halter, thought Senior, his hands clutching, clenching and fizzing around Margot's perky firm breasts and zinging nipples, his hips twitching spasmodically under the polished cherrywood table covered with shattered walnut shells, underneath that halter lightly down with golden fuzz I want to eat to eat to eat.

And Senior Hollinday zapped a fantasy Margot in a safe warm motel room lined with brocade and mirrors and banquet tables heaped high with buns and buns and buns and tall fast-food hamburgers and French-fried potatoes and deep-fried corn fritters with huge tubs full of Special Sauce loaded into transcontinental freight trucks and shipped all over North America and even the world while cool smooth Margot thrashed in unspeakable ecstasy under Senior's immensely sleek and powerful body performing with such splendour and kinky skill on the black satin sheets of his imagination as he mushroomed throbbing behind the tightly zippered fly of his immaculate grey business suit.

He lunged forward to grab a double armful of walnut shells and pulled them all off the table into his lap in one terrible wheezing thrust and then looked up at Wild Bill and said in a calm, unruffled voice, 'What happened?'

'I don't know,' said Judge Carter. 'You had some kind of fit there for about ten minutes. You sounded like a tea-kettle wheezing like that. Are you all right now?'

'I guess so. My God, that's never happened to me before, but I've been under a lot of strain lately, you know. The business, things going so well and then . . .'

Wild Bill thought he understood. Government trouble. That's what this country gets for putting the Democrats in power. Things start falling apart. That war in Asia and the government snooping on honest citizens.

'Sure I know,' he said. 'Damn government snooping around honest citizens like that. No wonder you're under a strain. You ought to take a few weeks off, get a rest. Go fishing or something.'

'Well,' said Senior, 'in a week or so I drive out to my lodge in Idaho. I'll get some rest there.' Thinking, Oh God, how can I get Margot into the front seat of my Couple de Ville and take her away with me to the wild mountains of Idaho, ho, ho.

32

Bobalou picked Orville up at five the day of their first date.

'I'd like to pluck your Magic Twanger, Froggy,' she said as soon as he slid into the front seat of her 1974 Dodge van. Orville had never met such a candid woman.

Bobalou shifted into First, popped the clutch, and the van squealed across the concrete apron of the Li'l Injun station towards Highway 30 accompanied by a shout of 'Ooooo-weee' from the office. Orville looked back and saw Slim slapping his thigh with his Stetson and grinning like a shark in rut before the station disappeared behind the swirling curtain of snow still falling straight down from the vaulted Wyoming sky on to the deepening virginal silence of the countryside.

Bobalou slowed down when she reached the highway, and they drove through the small chapel of their visible world without talking, the limits of their lives only a few feet away, tyres whispering a devotion to the snow on the road.

She guided the van on to a dirt road and finally parked in what seemed to be a huge nave of trees divided by the purled swish of the Little Muddy River.

'I've got dinner,' said Bobalou, breaking the fast of silence that had gripped them both. She led Orville into the back of the van, where she set up two folding chairs on either side of a small table. Orville noticed the water bed, the imitation fur, the candle on the table, the folded snowy-white paper napkins.

She pushed a button, and a stereo cassette recorder played Andre Kostelanetz's 1001 Strings softly into the warm yellow light from the candle. The curtains were open on the back windows of the van, but there was nothing to see but the dark grey flecks of snow falling through the gathering evening.

Orville thought about Buster Brown, living in a shoe with his dog. It must be like this, he thought, surrounded by the safety of the shoe, no one knows you're there,

Just the two

Of you.

He thought about Froggy the Gremlin. I'm Froggy the

Gremlin, he thought, and he thought about his Magic Twanger that Bobalou wanted to pluck. Bobalou removed small white cartons with wire handles, the kind Orville used to bring goldfish home in, from a paper bag and put them on the table. Then she got out two sets of chopsticks, and Orville realized they were going to have Chinese food from Young Foo's Chow Mein Palace.

Orville had never tasted anything so good in his life. He sat at the table and dribbled fried rice and egg roll down the front of the blue work shirt he wore under his Li'l Injun coveralls and stared at Bobalou's lips as they worked their way around the two wooden chopsticks, sucking from their tips small balls of rice or pieces of chicken, water chestnuts, palm hearts, black mushrooms, bean sprouts, green pepper. He watched her tongue flick out its tender tip and clean the sticks of the last vestiges of warm sauce. He dropped an egg roll in his lap and quickly grabbed it with his fingers and popped it into his mouth without taking his eyes from Bobalou's face. He thought he was in love.

After dinner they smoked a joint and lay down on the fur rug and stared at the ceiling of the van flickering with candlelight in time to the strains of Andre Kostelanetz while the snow fell and fell through the leafless cottonwoods and into the sibilant waters of the Little Muddy River, and finally, although Orville wasn't exactly a virgin, he might as well have been.

33

When Mary Lou Perkins first went out with Orville and rode with him up to Eden Park to see the view, and didn't look at the view at all, and later got arrested, she wasn't exactly a virgin either, but she didn't exactly know that, either.

Mary Lou had, in fact, five years, two months and six days before dating Orville, lost her virginity to her twin brother, Frank, and had been screwing him ever since. But that wasn't sex, she thought. Mary Lou grew up in the days when sex was a matter for the House Un-American Activities Committee and couldn't be talked about without dire consequences. All she knew was that sex was something you weren't supposed to let men do to you, and what she and Frank did was what she and Frank always did. It was fun; therefore it couldn't be sex.

They had discovered screwing in Roomette 36, Car 1493, of a Pennsylvania Railroad sleeper en route from New York to Florida, where they were going to visit Aunt Mildred, a widow of means with a house on the water in Palm Beach and a trim fifty-five-foot sloop with a permanent, full-time crew, including a young, very handsome, completely incompetent captain.

Frank and Mary Lou were thirteen years old; their parents were in a stateroom in the next car having an argument. Mr Perkins was maintaining that it might be harmful to the children to find out about Aunt Mildred's peculiar living arrangements with the young captain. Mrs Perkins, to whom Aunt Mildred belonged by right of blood, stated that there was nothing whatever to the rumours that Mr Perkins may have heard. Furthermore, Aunt Mildred was a widow of means and could live her life any way she wanted to. On top of which she had all the money in the family, and if Mr Perkins wanted to continue to live in the manner to which he had become accustomed, then he had better be damn nice to Aunt Mildred and not say anything about her, so there. It was an irrefutable argument and Mr Perkins had no reply, so he strode manfully through the swaying train to the club car.

Meanwhile, Frank and Mary Lou had shrugged out of their clothes and were surprised to notice certain anatomical alterations since the last time they had travelled together. Frank, one hand steadying himself on the edge of the upper berth, his Jockey shorts around his ankles, was looking down in mild chagrin at his quivering adolescent erection when Mary Lou, naked herself by now, noticed this fascinating phenomenon and reached forward with a giggle to give it a rub. This prompted Frank to ask, 'Well, what about yours?' and fondle her sweetening dampness, and pretty soon, well, they found if he put *his* in *hers*, there they were, and there was no reason they knew of to stop.

Then, a few weeks before Mary Lou went out with Orville, Frank announced his engagement to a girl named Muffy Schmidlapp, whose father was a psychiatrist and who was seventy-three days pregnant. Mary Lou felt completely betrayed, and decided that if Frank could go out and have sex with someone, then she could damn well do the same, so she said yes to Orville, having made up her mind that she was going to stop being a virgin that very night.

Orville picked her up at seven. Mr Perkins, who was deeply preoccupied with his wife's Aunt Mildred's failing health at the time, asked Orville only the most perfunctory questions and told him to bring Mary Lou home by midnight.

They went to see *Gigi*, a very romantic movie, and while Orville was trying to figure out how to introduce the matter of visiting the park to look at the view into the homeward conversation, Mary Lou was trying to calculate exactly how far to sit from Orville in the front seat of his 1958 Ford Edsel convertible to indicate that she wanted to go to the park for some sex, whatever that was, without frightening him off.

Orville made a wrong turn. 'Oh, gosh,' he said. 'I made a wrong turn.'

'Oh, well,' said Mary Lou with, could it be, relief? 'We have time yet before I have to get home. Where does this road go?'

They both knew perfectly well where it went.

'I think it goes to Eden Park,' said Orville.

'Gosh,' said Mary Lou, thinking that all might yet go well.

They parked up there under the clouds, and within minutes the windows were steamed up, which made Mary Lou think they were safe and Orville wonder whether he should open a window or put down the top. He did neither.

Mary Lou tried to maintain a balance between sexual aggression and feigned reluctance. So did Orville. He started by telling her of his dream to own his own gas pump in Little America.

Mary Lou melted into his arms. 'Gee,' she said.

Soon they were in the back seat working their way towards the real thing when Orville got sidetracked about killing his father and Mary Lou got distracted by the sensations in her groin (sensations by now familiar).

Then, as the car moved down the slope towards Officer Quint, she started to think about her rotten brother Frank and how he had betrayed her.

34

Frank Perkins became a Green Beret because his wife, Muffy, ran off with a saxophone player from Reading, Pennsylvania. She met him at a small jazz club to which Frank had taken her two years after their son, Henry, was born.

Frank thought he was a terrible saxophone player and was sure that couldn't be what Muffy saw in him. Frank couldn't imagine what Muffy saw in him.

Frank went through Basic Training, and Advanced Infantry Training, and Jump School, and Guerrilla Warfare Training, and Underwater Demolition Training, and Unarmed Combat Training, and Dirty Tricks Training, and became an expert with every deadly weapon in the army arsenal from helicopter gunship to thumb and forefinger. Then he went through Jungle Survival Training, and Desert Survival Training, and learned how to live off the land in the Arctic, and how to swim underwater up Haiphong Harbour and drill small holes in the bottoms of Communist gunboats, and how to make an electronic torture device out of a field telephone and a flashlight battery to get information out of reluctant prisoners.

And Frank learned about dope.

It was part of his training, a special programme of his unit, to get the enemy addicted and so buzzed out they would be unable to fight. The programme was ultimately unsuccessful.

In fact, it backfired.

Before he shipped out to Vietnam, Frank had a conversation with his father's good friend Senior Hollinday.

'Keep your eyes open over there,' Senior advised. 'There's plenty of opportunity for the right person in a conflict like this. The Communists are one thing, and they must be stopped of course, but business is business, and if there is an opportunity, it should be taken. That's what made this country the greatest nation the world has ever seen, and what will keep it that way,' Senior paused to sip his Scotch and water.

Frank held his five-foot four-inch muscular body, the shortest in the Green Berets, perfectly erect in his chair in the Walnut

Room of the country club. A shot glass full of bourbon and a glass of beer sat in front of him.

'Yes, sir,' he said. He tossed his head back and dropped the bourbon into his open mouth. Then he leaned forward slightly to sip his beer and sat up straight again.

Senior admired him greatly.

'As you know,' Senior continued, 'I manufacture pharmaceuticals for the military. I also make food products, specifically fastfoods, which as you no doubt realize are catching on like crazy. One of the things that makes me successful in a highly competitive business like wholesaling fastfoods is that I use only the best ingredients. Particularly in my Special Sauce. Some of those ingredients are imported. I use only the very best.'

'Yes, sir.'

'One of the most important ingredients comes from Asia. I have a lot of contacts over there. Perhaps when you have finished with your work pacifying the country and so forth, you might be interested in pursuing a few things for me. It could be a real opportunity for you, a chance to make some real money.'

Frank was not really going to Vietnam to pacify anyone. Frank was going to Vietnam because his wife, Muffy, ran off with a saxophone player, and had taken their son, Henry, with her. And because his sister, Mary Lou, had been arrested as accessory to assault with a deadly weapon with Senior's son Orville, and there was actually nothing to keep him at home.

Senior's offer sounded very promising, though a thin thread of suspicion twisted redly up Frank's spine about the Special Sauce ingredient Senior hinted at.

Frank decided to have another bourbon with beer chaser, just to toast Senior and his new job.

35

Elmo Laurel, MSGT, USA Ret., returned to his hometown after retiring from the army with twenty years of retirement benefits and no obligations and hung around with his brother Edward for a few weeks. He quickly became bored.

'Ed,' he said over a Seven and Seven at a downtown bar

called Nick's on Culvert Road, 'I'm forty-eight years old, it is the winter of nineteen seventy-four, I got army benefits, I know how to make masses of food for thousands and I'm getting bored with bowling. I think I'll get a job.'

'OK, Elmo, whatever you say.' Edward was slumped into his seat next to the jukebox, an obsolete Wurlitzer that played the same Frankie Avalon record over and over at unpredictable intervals. Edward thought the machine must have a life of its own. He'd never seen anyone put any money in it.

At the moment he was not thinking about the Wurlitzer, though. He wasn't thinking at all; he was slipping gently into unconsciousness, a place warm and safe as a swimming pool full of béchamel sauce, a place where he was untroubled by his hatred of his job at the country club and his envy of his older brother's independence.

'Yes,' said Elmo, unaware of his brother's departure, 'I'll get a job.' He was sipping his seventh Seven and Seven, but showed no effects other than a certain loquaciousness. 'I spent twenty years in the good old US Army, sixteen of them on the same base, a place full of atomic bombs and weirdo skinny officers, making delicious food for both enlisted men and officers. I know all about food. Just like you, Ed.' He nodded towards Ed's body, his eyes on a world in which food was king, and he was prime minister.

Elmo got up and walked steadily into the men's room, a small cardboard shell lit by fluorescent ultraviolet tubes with a glowing pink urinal. A life-sized black-light poster of Raquel Welch in a jungle bikini from a movie called *One Billion Years BC* covered the wall in front of him.

Behind him, next to the sink, the head of a department store mannequin with a red wig and a name tag, MONA, smirked at him. Nick, whose real name was Art Foster, had some strange ideas about lavatory décor. He had lavished special care on the ladies' room; the result was that patrons only seemed to use it once. Edward, who spent a lot of time at Nick's, got a tour one quiet afternoon when he was the only customer and could well understand why.

Elmo peed and peered around in the violet gloom. He could just make out some of the remarks his predecessors had written on the walls. Most of them delineated fantasy activities with the department store dummy beside the sink, one of which directed Elmo's eyes to her mouth, which someone had suggestively

64

outlined with Helena Rubenstein number 76, Crimson Sin.

In front of Mona's face, looking as if she had just released it from her mouth like faithful Rover, was a folded newspaper. Elmo took it back to his table.

In the want ad section, which he spread out after handing Ed the sports page, he found:

We need an experienced man who knows food, especially sauces. Apply in person, Hollinday Industrial Pharmaceuticals, Warren G. Harding Industrial Park, Personnel Dept. Good pay, opportunity for advancement.

'Sounds like just the job for me,' said Elmo. 'Look, Ed, the perfect job for me.'

Ed didn't answer.

36

Frank Perkins, pacifier of more dinks than anyone else in his unit, didn't answer the small man next to him.

Frank only knew a few words of Cambodian, for one thing, although his Vietnamese was good. And for another thing, Frank was stoned out of his mind. In that mind John Wayne led a commando attack on a hamlet of huts made of wood and rice straw. 'Well, men,' drawled the Duke, 'that town is full of Charlies an' it's our job ta go in there an' get 'em out!'

The village was burning satisfactorily and scores of tiny, black-clad figures, shorter than Frank, scurried in all directions into the brush. The machine-guns were going like crazy, and the forest was lit up with the quick hot flicker of napalm, and John Wayne's face was streaked with sweat and a gleaming, euphoric smile. Frank was doing in Commie after Commie with neat sideways strokes of the edge of his palm to their fragile necks. The whole thing was very exciting and reminded Frank in a peculiar way of his sister Mary Lou.

The little man next to him spoke again. They were sitting in a small clearing about seventeen kilometres from the Mekong River on the Cambodian side. Both wore black pyjamas and large conical straw hats. Frank held a long opium pipe, which now drooped from his dreamy fingers.

'What'd you say?' he asked in Vietnamese.

The man repeated it a third time.

'Oh, yes,' said Frank. 'Good. Yes, good. Very good.' He said it in Cambodian. 'How much?'

The man spoke again, and Frank caught the words 'kilo' and 'dollars'. 'Fifty dollars a kilo?' he asked. 'That's good. Very good. But how much? How much . . . get?'

'Ahh. Understand.' The man smiled, revealing a mouthful of rotten stumps. The smile had a strange, corrupt charm – he too was stoned, though not as stoned as Frank. They had been sampling the sticky substance wrapped in brown paper at their feet, and things seemed to be going well. 'One hundred kilos,' the man said carefully.

'Good,' said Frank.

Frank was engaged on a secret mission for his government. He had killed or 'pacified' as it was termed, three hundred and seventeen enemy soldiers, of all ages and sexes, and been awarded a number of important combat medals, including the coveted Body Count Award for the highest average per month. He had been awarded as well a field commission and was now a first lieutenant. It seemed likely, if he kept up his average, he would make captain within the month. Frank knew that would never happen, though.

The secret mission entrusted to him by his government was called Operation Helping Hand; the name was a cover, designed to look like a Red Cross operation. The government was trying to give a helping hand to the opium traffic among the Viet Cong. Millions in unaccountable funds were diverted into this project. The Viet Cong were completely uninterested.

Frank was not at all uninterested. He knew the knock of opportunity and had volunteered. Senior had advised him to keep his eyes open, and he had. Opportunity knocked and then laid down a long trail from Saigon to this small clearing near a nameless village in Cambodia, where Frank was having a chat with the village headman.

'One hundred kilos,' said Frank. 'Refined opium. Each year.'

The village headman nodded, and somewhere behind Frank's eyes John Wayne patted him on the back for the good job he'd done.

'Good. Very good,' said Frank.

37

'What we're interested in,' Eggs began. He and Orville had left the Coffee Shoppe and were walking back to Orville's room.

Little America had been almost completely redecorated in red, white and blue in honour of the Fourth of July. Orville had even admonished Eggs for ordering an egg salad sandwich instead of a Ben Franklin. All the sandwiches at the Coffee Shoppe had historic names like that.

'What we're interested in is someone to sort of be our agent here in Little America. Keep track of trucking of atomic materials, particularly weapons-grade stuff. You know, kind of keep an eye out, work up some monthly averages, file a report say once a month or so. Maybe do a little investigating of security precautions now and then. Wouldn't take much time, only a couple of hours every month. We'd pay well, you know. We need someone with some experience with fissionables. And a security clearance. How about it?'

Yes, Orville thought he might be interested. How much would it pay, though? And when would he have to start? Would they give him a contract?

A great deal, immediately, and yes, Eggs told him. 'And I'll throw in a free copy of *The Jesus Connection*.' Eggs laughed. 'It's all about how to get hooked on Jesus.'

'Well,' said Orville, 'I'm in a transcendental meditation study group right now, and I'm not sure it's really the thing for me, but I certainly wouldn't turn down a free copy. There's not too much to read in Little America, you know. No library. The Gifte Shoppe does have a book rack, but it doesn't sell *The Jesus Connection* as far as I know. I did buy a book called *Gang Bang* there.'

The members of the Paradise Lost Motorcycle Club circled her helpless, half-naked body, smiling cruelly. Cherry squirmed, weak with fear, but the ropes that held her wrists tied to the handlebars of the leader's big Harley were tied too tight. She tried to kick out at the one the others called Punch, but he danced out of the way, laughing, mocking her. The leader slowly unzipped his fly and took out his enormous –

'What'd you say?' Orville's mind had wandered, so he missed Eggs's question.

'I said, "What have you been doing all these years?"'

'Oh. Mostly I spent five years as a law clerk for a judge at home. He worked on legislation about atomic materials, in fact. The army was trying to take all radioactive material away from civilians and private industry and stockpile it themselves. But it didn't work of course. Industry is too well established now, too much money in it, I guess. My cousin Owen owns a company that uses radioactive material. I've sort of lost track of all that since I've been out here.'

'Yeah,' said Eggs. 'I remember that bill. It had the agency worried for a time, but the industry lobby was too strong, as you say. And things haven't been going all that well for the military since Vietnam, so it's not too surprising it failed.'

'Anyway there are a lot of Nader types around who worry about security, and that's money for you and me, eh?' Eggs was still the same, he still looked out for Eggs.

'Well,' said Orville. 'This is where I live.'

38

'Take me home.'

Flora Hollinday had just had her first date with Andrew Winkler. She sat in the front seat of his pale green 1962 Lincoln Continental with dark green leather upholstery and windows that slid up and down at the touch of a panel button on the driver's side. They were parked in back of a half-built Kernel Korn's Drive-In Restaurant just off the Louisa May Alcott Freeway near Riverdale Avenue. Because of a plumbers' strike, no one was nearby.

The seats were also hydraulic, and Flora's was tilted back seventy-two degrees from the vertical. Her imitation Givenchy spring frock was clustered coquettishly around her white dimpled thighs, and Andrew Winkler, breathing stentoriously through his prominent nose, was trying to manoeuvre that organ past Flora's neatly turned knees into the aromatic folds of the fake

Givenchy, which she had bought at Bergdorf Goodman's in New York City for $169.99, plus tax.

'Take me home,' she said again. Her hand rested lightly on Mr Winkler's small round bald spot, and she was finding the air in the Continental rather close.

'Eh? What?' After a casual meeting in the street, Andrew had driven her out to show her his one hundred and thirty-seventh Kernel Korn's; he was aggreieved that construction was being held up by the plumbers' strike, but he was very proud that he had built up his chain of fast-food restaurants from nothing but the one original hamburger stand and the two hundred and fifty thousand dollars his father had loaned him.

'We can't do this, Andrew. It's not right.' Flora tried to put real conviction into her voice to convince Mr Winkler, her husband's friend, that what they were doing was wrong. But her words sounded watery even to her.

'What about your wife?' she ventured. Her hand slipped down across the bald spot, over the short black hairs on the back of his head, and her fingers dipped into the narrow space between his collar and neck, as though testing the temperature there.

Andrew's wife, Babs, short for Barbara, had long ago blended her stout torso into the rich panelling of his suburban life so effectively that he no longer noticed her. He didn't exactly ignore her, for he would answer when she asked a question, respond when she wanted something, but he did it vacantly, the same way he watered his lawn or waxed his car. He would be capable, two years later, of standing next to her at his daughter Bobo's (short for Barbara) coming-out party, while they greeted the guests, and being aware of her only as an inert mass next to him.

So when Flora asked, 'What about your wife?' it took Andrew a moment to (1) understand *what* she had said, and (2) figure out *who* she was talking about. His nose stopped its probing until he figured it all out. As soon as he had done so, he forgot all about it.

'Ummmm. Ne'er min'.' He was forcing his left eye down between Flora's knees as far as it would go. By squinting, he obtained a strained glimpse of her white panties snugged up under the folds of the peach-coloured print dress. His nose was twitching.

Flora got a feeling that the nose might be a motif, a pattern that could be repeated somewhere lower down. She was sure that it would be very nice to find out if that were so, but of course that was out of the question, it was unthinkable, she shouldn't think it.

But the afternoon was warm, the grass was beginning to colour the vacant lot around the construction site with the first tentative green of spring, and insects were droning in the crab-grass.

'Oh, Andrew,' she said, gripping his wonderful nose tightly between her knees. 'Please take me home!'

39

About the time Slim was having his elbow bent back at a ninety-degree angle in front of him, so he looked like an offensive guard protecting the runner of quarterback, and encased in plaster of paris, Owen was sliding down the cab of his Mack diesel in a luminous mist of sexual afterglow and walking over to the Li'l Injun station to tell his cousin Orville all about it.

'Jesus, Orville,' he said when he walked into the grimy office where Orville, leaning against the Coke machine, gazed at the empty lube rack. There was the usual midmorning lull in the tourist traffic. This was one of those peculiar, balmy desert days with low clouds rolling eastward a thousand feet over their heads. 'Jesus, Orville!'

'Pretty good?' said Orville. He was feeling lazy and replete. He had, the night before, successfully purloined four canisters of fissionable material from Owen's truck and replaced the bird-cages, as the shock-absorbing frameworks housing the canisters were called, filled with sand. It would be a long time, he was sure, before the thefts were detected.

'Jesus, Orville,' Owen said a third time. 'I thought I was a goner.' He told Orville about his adventure with Juanita and Slim's dramatic entrance, and what happened after Slim knocked himself out. 'It was terrific,' he concluded.

'Why don't I close up for a while, and we can get some breakfast before you leave.' Orville hung the CLOSED sign in the window, and they walked over to the Coffee Shoppe.

Orville wasn't certain, but maybe the Coffee Shoppe was that very place where he had eaten a hamburger when he was nine years old.

'I'd like a General Sherman, and my friend will have a Ulysses S. Grant Special.' Although ten years had passed since the centennial celebration of the Civil War, the Coffee Shoppe had retained a number of the menu entries commemorating that event. Orville was actually eating a Spanish omelet, which looked, presumably, like the end result of the March to the Sea. Including the burning of Atlanta (chilli sauce). Owen was having fried eggs sunnyside up. Perhaps they looked like General Grant's eyes.

'But why,' Orville asked Owen over the remains of breakfast, 'are you driving that truck?'

'Well, you know, since Dad died . . .'

Orville murmured something solemn, sharing the grief.

'. . . we're still making parts for jet engines for the military, but we're branching out. Dad would never do that, you know, but it's important these days to diversify. Times have changed, you know. Fissionable materials are the coming thing, nuclear power plants, military applications and so on. We have the engineering staff for it, so why not? We have built a breeder reactor in Idaho, making high-grade plutonium. It's all automated and everything, but we have to feed it, so I'm driving this refined U-235 out there. It's a sensitive shipment, and I didn't really want to trust it anyone else.

'Besides, frankly, I wanted to get away from the office. And away from Margot.'

40

Margot had matured since her wedding to Owen.

Her body, which then had seemed to be stuffed with millions of tiny balls of some springy elastic substance that zipped around inside her skin as though each one were highly charged with static electricity, had now blossomed, had opened up like a perfect American Beauty rose; she was full, compact and sweet. She smelled like a hillside in the Tehachapi Mountains in spring when the wildflowers were in bloom.

She was, at the very moment her husband made his first tentative spelunk into Janita's unmapped interior, stretching her ivory arms above her head in the luxury of her solitude.

Of course she was not really alone. Trembling at her living-room window in a heated frenzy of peeping was Senior Hollinday, who since the wedding had been eating his heart out, forced to be content with only such crumbs as Margot deigned to scatter in his path, a path that slurped along behind her like a sweaty damp shadow.

Margot was a moving diagram of economy of movement. No muscle moved more than was absolutely necessary as she drifted from room to room in the house like the soft breeze of a perfectly functioning air-conditioning system, making the place neat. When she lifted her arms above her head and stretched, squeezing her hands together, her perfect chest lifted in inverse exponential proportion to the sinking sensation in Senior's throat and stomach.

Because she was alone and the drapes were drawn, she wore only a pair of patterned, pastel panties. So Senior, who had found the one chink in the living-room curtains by moving his eye slowly over every square inch of glass on the first floor of the house like Sherlock Holmes with a magnifying glass until he located it, and who had then clamped his eye to that spot as firmly as a burglar's rubber suction cup, saw in full view this entire gesture, elbows straightening, hands arching over her head, the pink nipples lifting quizzically, and could stand it no more.

He was wearing his best suit, so he crouched awkwardly to keep his knees out of the dirt of the bed of daffodils under the picture window. He pulled his eye away from the glass with an almost audible pop, removed from his jacket pocket his pair of aggressively masculine horn-rimmed glasses, smoothed back his wavy, silvered hair, and edged around to the front of the house and rang the front doorbell. He knew it was too much to ask, but he hoped she'd answer the door the way she was.

There was a long wait, a disappointment he could almost taste. He carefully rehearsed what he would say. His car was parked two blocks away. It had broken down. Could he use her phone? he would ask. She would offer him a drink. They would sit together on the couch, chatting idly of this and that. He would be handsome and gentle and persuasive and soon, he could *really* taste it, he would be within reach of his heart's desire, he would pluck (he could feel it) the exquisite flower of his niece. He would take off his glasses with a commanding gesture, drape his immaculate suited arm around her shoulders, and kiss her: fatherly at first, but soon a lover.

He rang the bell again, his hand beginning to shake a little. Maybe she wasn't going to answer the door?

Finally, after two eternities, Margot opened the door and stood before him fully dressed. 'Well,' she said. 'Senior. How are you?'

'My bar has croaked,' he told her. 'I'd like to fuck your phone.'

41

When Senior had dropped off his small son Orville at Camp Tomahawk that pleasant June in fifty-three, he drove on alone to a ranch near the small town of Squash, Idaho. At one time the local farmers had hoped that their region would become one of the great acorn squash-growing areas of the world. So when something like a town developed, they named it Squash.

The soil there was entirely unsuited to the raising of acorn squash, and most of the farmers went broke and drifted on, but the town lingered like one of Chuckie Chipwood's terminal kidney patients, from back when he lived and worked in Billings, Montana.

The Hay There Ranch, object of Senior's drive, raised mainly hay of a slightly inferior kind. It belonged to a retired broker from Hackensack, New Jersey, who had been a friend of Senior's father; he'd once had relatives in Goshen, Indiana, and used to rent bicycles from Grandfather Hollinday.

As Senior drove up the dusty road to the ranch house, he noticed the retired broker, whose name was Stan, sitting in a chair on the front porch amid a welter of rustic junk. A large pair of antlers from an animal not indigenous to the region (which Stan had bought at an auction in Hackensack) loomed over the door. Stan liked to affect an authentic Western demeanour when he was in Idaho, which was now all the time, so he would clear his throat and spit on occasion, something he had never done in Hackensack. It was an odd gesture for someone wearing a bright green plaid suit.

Senior parked his Cadillac in a swirl of reddish dust and climbed out. 'Howdy, Senior,' said Stan, after a pause to clear his throat and spit in a long arc off the porch. 'How long can you stay? Fran!' he shouted without waiting for an answer. 'Senior's here!'

He shouted it straight at Senior, though it was clear that Fran must be somewhere inside the house. Before she could answer Stan said to Senior in a normal tone, 'Fran's inside making some kind of country pudding. Can't understand why she keeps trying, it always turns out lousy; she's a lousy cook, terrible. She'll be out in a minute.'

Fran appeared in the doorway, and for a moment it looked to Senior as though the antlers were growing directly from her wizened head. 'Why, Senior,' she said without the faintest hint of a smile on a face caught in the middle of endless collapse. 'How wonderful to see you.'

Later on Senior had to eat the country pudding, which was truly awful. Then he offered Stan a cigar to dispel the lingering taste, and the two of them sat on the porch and listened for a spell to the hay growing. It was warm, and the cigar smoke rose aromatically straight into the night. Insects chirped and warbled, and from time to time in the distance an owl would hoot. Overhead the stars drew closer and brighter than they ever were in Hackensack, New Jersey. Mountain and water smells enveloped the house in a peace outside of time.

Senior told Stan about the Special Sauce he was beginning to manufacture. Stan understood. That's what made this country great, he said. He told Senior it was admirable to spot opportunity like that and take advantage. Senior told Stan he admired *him*, the way he had turned the stock market crash of twenty-nine into a fortune, and Stan replied that there was always an opportunity to make money in times like those. And these, for that matter, he added, with the war in Korea and Communists everywhere.

And Senior told Stan that he was looking around for a hunting lodge, a place to get away from it all.

So while Orville thrashed his way through his first miserable night at Camp Tomahawk, his father and Stan were thrashing out how much Senior would pay for the cabin with ten acres that Stan just happened to have available on the back side of his ranch near Squash, Idaho.

42

Orville tried never to dwell on the manly virtues that his six summers at Camp Tomahawk had instilled in him. He usually succeeded.

'I hated it,' he told his room-mate at Yale Law School, who was still lying on the imitation Persian rug in their apartment. It was one of the rare occasions when he failed to repress memories of Camp Tomahawk. They had smoked a bit more of the Acapulco special, and Orville noticed distantly that Bert's red hair almost matched one of the colours in the rug. Bert's blue eyes stared unwaveringly at the ceiling. Every now and then he said 'Yeah' very softly.

'I hated it. They had cute rustic log cabins that reeked of damp and bugs, and a dammed-off swimming hole full of leeches, and a flagpole in front of the lodge where they made you stand out at dawn in your camp uniform while they raised the flag and made you pledge allegiance. They played a recording of a bugle playing "Taps" at bedtime. The counsellors were all older boys with great ideas about discipline. Like my father whom I'm going to kill when I get out of here. And then I'm going to get a gas pump in Little America, like I said.'

Orville didn't notice that he was repeating himself, or that Bert's eyes were gradually closing. To Bert, the ceiling of the room tilted majestically left, stopped, jerked a little every time the water dripped in the kitchen sink, and then changed direction and tilted to the right.

The word 'Tomahawk' had triggered something in his head, and he stood on a vast carpet in the middle of a line of plastic cowboys who rode plastic horses with soft legs that always bent in the wrong places. In front of him a row of Indians appeared over the edge of the coffee table. Bert thought this might be a good opportunity to apply what he had just learned in torts, but he wasn't quite sure how. It didn't seem to matter.

'Most of all,' Orville finished, 'it was the fishing. I sure did hate the fishing. I was a great fisherman, even won the fishing trophy the first year. I could throw in an empty hook and some

75

large trout would grab it with his mouth and I'd have to haul it in and then *kill* it and then *clean* it and then that night I'd have to *cook* it and then for Christ's sake I would have to *eat* it.'

Bert was a fish, swimming through the Persian carpet. 'I haven't been able to eat fish since then,' said Orville. 'The third year I dropped my fishing rod over the side of the canoe. I didn't have to fish again that summer, but the next year my father gave me a fly rod and I had to learn how to tie flies, bright pretty little things with hooks in them. I even taught fly-tying in shop to some of the younger kids. Ooooh, boy, Camp Tomahawk.'

Bert had never gone to camp. He had played basketball during the summers at the Y. Listening to Orville, he was glad he hadn't gone to camp, though if it had been a basketball camp it might have been a lot of fun. A brawny, naked Indian with the head of a fish swam at Bert dribbling a basketball. Bert popped his eyes open and the Indian disappeared. Perhaps there was a lawsuit here? Where was liability in a case like this?

Orville forgot about Camp Tomahawk. He started thinking about Bobo Winkler's coming-out party, and how he had drained the brake fluid from his father's car.

Then he fell asleep.

43

Master Sergeant Elmo Laurel, USA Ret., was wide awake as he wheeled his old 1967 Chevrolet Impala off the Louisa May Alcott Freeway into the parking lot at the east end of the Warren G. Harding Industrial Park. He got out and walked over to the gate set into the chain-link fence marked HIP INC., VISITORS ENTRANCE. Eight strands of barbed wire stretched between the tops of the fence posts. A guard in the little hut beside the gate gave him a visitor's pass and directed him to the personnel office.

This is really something, Elmo thought. Just like the army.

The personnel director, a small bald man in crepe-soled shoes, bounded up and down on his toes as he shook hands with the applicant. It appeared as though he thought this motion might make him somewhat taller, at least half the time. 'So you've come about the ad in the paper,' he said as he sat down behind his desk. Suddenly, he did seem taller. A nameplate on his desk said he was Mr Steckbeck. He drank eight ounces of carrot juice each day, which he made at home in an electric juicer.

'That's right,' said Elmo. 'Frankly, it seems as if the job were made for me.'

Mr Steckbeck tented his fingers in front of his face and tilted back in his chair; it screeched horribly. 'Hmmmm,' he said. 'Well, we'll see about that.'

He bounced the chair back two or three times, producing a sound like a surgical saw cutting through a skull. Then he lunged forward suddenly, placed his hands flat on the desk, and asked, 'What makes you think so?' He stared straight at Elmo.

Sergeant Laurel was not bothered by this manoeuvre. He had practised it often enough in the army. So he told Mr Steckbeck why he was qualified.

Mr Steckbeck was delighted. In front of him on the desk was a memo from Senior Hollinday himself outlining the necessary qualifications for the job that had no title as yet, and it did indeed seem as though this man had been trained especially for it.

But Mr Steckbeck didn't say so. Instead, he administered a battery of tests to Elmo. He gave him the Stanford-Binet Intelligence Test. Then he showed Elmo the pictures in the Thematic Apperception Test and asked him to make up stories about them. He gave Elmo the MMPI and his own version of an SAT. He gave Elmo a one-hour written test in which he had to answer hundreds of questions about himself that got confusing because the same questions kept popping up in different phrasings, and Elmo had no time to check how he had answered earlier. Finally Mr Steckbeck asked him to wait in the waiting-room.

Elmo had almost finished *Reader's Digest* before Mr Steckbeck called him back into the office. 'We need a man of proven ambition and loyalty,' he told Elmo. 'A man with a knowledge of foods and a sense of discipline. A man of proven leadership capability who knows how to handle people. And we need a man who knows how to keep his mouth shut. From your tests I'd say you'll do nicely. Congratulations.'

'Thank you,' said Elmo without surprise.

He and Mr Steckbeck stared at one another for a long moment. Finally the personnel director said, 'Well?'

'There's just one thing I'd like to know,' said Elmo.
'What's that?'
'What am I supposed to do?'

44

'What did you do before you became a uranium marshal?'
Orville asked.

He and Eggs were sitting in Orville's room in Little America.
Eggs sat in the chair and Orville sat on the bed. Behind Eggs
was a huge poster of a minuteman looking dedicated and sincere
over which was printed in italic script the opening paragraphs
of the Declaration of Independence. At the bottom of the
poster, just visible above the back of the chair, was the an-
nouncement that for over two hundred years Americans had
had the inalienable liberty of protecting themselves and their
loved ones with Bunker Hill Life Insurance.

'Well,' said Eggs, tenting his fingers together and staring
upwards at the ceiling. The minuteman's rifle pointed out over
his head. 'I was in the frozen pizza business. After the army I
got to hanging around in Houston, Texas, with a pizza freak
named Perry Bender. Met him in the park one day, smoking
some Rio Grande Blue, which he shared. We got to talking
about pizza, something I never was particularly interested in
before; he said Houston was a great pizza town. "Houston's a
great pizza town, you know," ' he said.

'So pretty soon there we were, pooling our resources, which
came to three hundred and fifty-eight dollars and an idea. The
idea was if we had the right gimmick the frozen pizza business
could be very profitable. Since health foods were just catching
on in Houston at the time, we decided to make a frozen organic
pizza. Wow. I mean, whole wheat flour and natural tomatoes.
Unprocessed cheese. Soybean sausage. Lots of lecithin. Frozen
organic pizza . . .' Eggs trailed off. He looked as though he still
couldn't believe he had done such a thing.

'You know, it caught on like crazy,' he began again. 'There
was a lot of pride down there – you know Texas – in having a
local brand, not some big New York corporation coming into

the supermarkets. We called it Neapolitan Natural Frozen Pizza. Within three years our little company was making two million dollars a year in gross sales. We both bought big houses and fancy cars. I had a twelve-cylinder Jaguar. That was in nineteen seventy-two or three.'

Eggs leaned his head back on to the minuteman's musket muzzle. 'It was incredible I tell you. You can't imagine how many people wanted to buy frozen pizza; we couldn't turn the stuff out fast enough.'

'But it all really depended on one big contract: we sold all the frozen pizza to the entire Houston school district. Every two weeks every pupil in Houston from kindergarten through high school would have a seventeen-cent slice of frozen pizza for lunch. Seven hundred and sixty-seven thousand dollars' worth every year. It was a terrific bargain for the school board; for a mere seventeen cents a slice a student got bread, vegetable, some protein and a dairy product. Throw in a little lettuce for greens and they had a whole meal for almost nothing.

'We made three cents on every slice. That meant all the Rio Grande Blue we wanted. And girls. We'd sit in our fancy office and drink champagne and smoke and laugh our asses off. I mean, *organic* frozen pizza. Incredible!' Eggs chuckled as he thought about it.

'Then it happened. The bubble burst. Of course it was too good to be true. A big company spotted what we were doing and moved in on the school board. Sold them frozen pizza for *thirteen* cents a slice, a terrific loss. Of course they could afford it. We tried selling it for twelve cents and lost everything. Had to go out of business.

'As soon as we folded, the big company raised its price to twenty cents. Now they're cleaning up.' He sighed.

'What happened to your partner?' asked Orville.

'Perry did all right. He went to work for the company that drove us out of business. I think it was his idea to charge twenty cents a slice.' Eggs shook his head. His expression almost matched that of the minuteman. 'He really knew the market. But I decided that business was not for me.'

45

Andrew Winkler's business was extracting his wide-flanged high-arched, cantilevered nose from between the creamy dimpled knees of Flora Hollinday, knees that surrounded and covered that nose like two dense, enormous marshmallows. He knew it was the hydraulic pressure of desire that pumped those knees together, not malice or wrath, but if he didn't break free soon he would suffocate.

A strange buzzing in his ears drowned out her pleas of 'Take me home,' but he wouldn't have understood even if he had heard her. He was beyond language; only sounds had meaning of a sort, and what he heard in her voice was not the ideational content of 'take' and 'home' but a hunger that matched his own. His view of her panties was blocked now, but it remained a vivid afterimage in his memory, so even as he struggled to free his nose and breathe, he strained to move it ever closer.

Suddenly he popped free of her knees and his head hurtled backwards against the bottom of the pale green dashboard of his Lincoln Continental. The buzzing in his ears turned to a roar and his vision fell into the damp vortex between Flora's legs and faded rapidly.

When he opened his eyes again, his head was just where he would have wanted it. Flora had opened his shirt and was stroking his chest with the same tender concern she displayed when she folded her son Orville's laundered underwear.

'Oh, Andrew, Andrew, are you all right?' she asked, her feeble urgency to be taken home fled before the flash flood of concern that flowed through her stomach and legs.

Andrew blinked once and stared into the pastel flowers crumpled two inches away from his face. A fold of the dress was gently draped across the bridge of his nose, placing that organ within centimetres of its objective. He felt a light tightness in his head and a powerful tightness in his beltless trousers. His nose twitched slightly, and Flora's hand, which had been smoothing the layer of fat over his ribs as though she were straightening the sheets on the imaginary Beauty Rest somewhere in the murky motel of her desire, now scurried, a white mouse that had studied for years with a metropolitan classical ballet troupe, for the waistband of his trousers, where with practiced dexterity it relieved the pressure.

At the very moment that Andrew's nose finally plunged the final fractions into the pure white fog of Flora's panties, the final button slipped from the buttonhole and he sprang forth from his pants into full view just beneath the hydraulically powered steering wheel of the Continental.

Flora felt a massive surge of weakness and gratitude sweep through her, behind the flood of concern, when she saw that the nose, which had begun to work with glorious power and promise, was indeed a harbinger, a herald, a clarion call to what was down below. Her hand closed around Andrew's shaft like a bank of thick evening fog around a lighthouse, and her eyes glazed, fixed on what she held, even as her legs fell open like a dictionary of dirty words.

Patrolman Hiram Quint, who had eased his squad car behind the unfinished Kernel Korn's to take a much-needed break from his arduous official duties, stood beside the Lincoln in a total stupor. His mouth hung slackly open and one of the early spring flies landed briefly on his mottled teeth.

What he saw in the car was carnage, a massacre of all that was decent and law-abiding. At last he pulled himself together and rapped firmly on the glass of Flora's window. 'What the hell's going on in there?' he croaked.

He never should have done that. It cost him his job.

46

Orville finally quit his job as Wild Bill Carter's law clerk because after almost five years it had become clear to everyone that Orville had neither an interest in nor an aptitude for the law, and would never make anything of himself in that field.

Senior of course was horrified. He was, however, so involved in his business affairs, and so preoccupied with his futile pursuit of Margot, that he didn't say anything directly to Orville about it.

He did talk to Margot, though. 'That no-good son of mine

will come to nothing, it seems,' he told her one day at lunch. 'Judge Carter mentioned to me that Orville doesn't even seem to be interested in helping draft the very important legislation he's working on. You'd think with his army experience and Yale Law School, for Christ's sake, he'd be perfectly qualified for it. He knows all about atomic weapons, too.'

Margot held a toothpick with an olive speared on it just in front of her mouth, but as long as Senior was talking she appeared to have forgotten about it because his conversation was so fascinating. Her large brown eyes gazed into his face with an expression that, had he not known better by now, he might have interpreted as adoration. When he stopped speaking for a moment, she opened her perfect mouth and closed her two dazzling rows of even white teeth on the olive. Senior could almost taste the exquisite crunch and burst of flavour. It all seemed to happen in extreme close-up and in slow motion.

To Margot, Senior's voice was a pleasant flow of sound. She was immediately and unthinkingly aware of the elegance of the restaurant, the muted clink of silverware and china, the almost surreptitious precision of the waiters, the discretion of the lighting that winked in highlights off the glassware, the unintelligible hum of conversations at near-by tables. Her daddy used to bring her here from time to time, and she floated on a warm bath of childhood security.

The place was far enough from town that they were not likely to run into anyone they knew, though of course there was nothing underhanded about their meeting. They were, after all, related. Nothing improper was going on.

That's what was driving Senior crazy. He knew this was a crumb, this luncheon that had just cost him thirty-seven dollars and sixty-nine cents. He looked mournfully a moment at Margot's half-empty wine glass. It still contained a dollar's worth of wine. Nothing improper will ever go on, he sulked. I am wearing new silk underwear and Margot will never see it.

'I just don't know quite what to do about Orville,' he said, thinking, I want to gobble those little wrists, those earlobes hidden in her hair. 'He's probably going to have to move over into some other kind of job, something more suited to his talents. He did quite well in law school, so I can't really understand this lack of interest.' It never occurred to Senior that Orville was serious when he had told him he wanted to go to Little America and have his own gas pump.

82

'Yes,' said Margot, her voice low, her eyes still resting on Senior's face. Voice and eyes registered concern, involvement, understanding, and Senior felt a thrill crackle through him even though he knew perfectly well that her eyes were really resting, that they had, in fact, gone on vacation.

Her body, recently perfected by her *Pinces de crabe aux anisette*, her *salade des coeurs de palmier*, her small dish of *sabayon froide* with *petits fours*, had indeed gone to some contented internal Florida for some sun, taking eyes and voice along for companionship, so she never remembered that Senior had asked her to speak to her husband Owen about a job for Orville in Owen's new Fission Division.

47

It never occurred to Orville that he might go to work for his cousin Owen. It was time, he felt, to move on to Little America, to at least satisfy that ambition. The other would wait.

He had a law degree, spoke fluent Russian, knew a great deal about atomic weapons, had experience writing legislation and some knowledge of automobiles (at least the parts one could wire bombs to). He was thirty years old, time to start a new career.

'It has become clear,' he told Wild Bill one day as the midwestern spring turned rancidly to summer, 'that my future does not lie precisely in being a lawyer. It may be in some related field. Business, perhaps. Or more likely, public service of some kind.'

Wild Bill nodded solemnly, a dignified personification of the judicious balance between pragmatism and existentialism. Actually, he was elated; his friend and patron's son, that small thorn on the rose of his life, was finally being plucked forever.

'I have deeply enjoyed working for you,' Orville lied with unabashed sincerity. 'I've learned a great deal about the workings of the law and the writing of legislation. It is certainly a difficult and rewarding profession, and were I a different person I'm sure I could have found my place in it.' Oddly enough, Orville felt this last to be true. 'I'll be leaving at the end of the month, if that's all right with you?'

'Well, Orville,' said Wild Bill, his wrinkled circular eyes revealing nothing of his inner self, but surely reflecting back to the world a covert malice, 'I'll certainly be sorry to see you go. You've done a wonderful job for me here, and I've never had any reason to question your devotion to your job or your competence at doing it. If you ever need a reference, or for that matter if you want to come back to work for me for any reason, why, the door is always open.' God forbid, thought the judge as he shook Orville's hand.

'By the way, what are you going to do?' he asked as he held the door open for Orville.

'I think I'll just take some time off, maybe travel around some, try to find myself. I'm sure that with a little time to think and look around, see what opportunities the world has to offer someone like me, I'll be able to figure something out, to settle on something where I have a real future.'

'I certainly do wish you the best of luck, Orville,' said Wild Bill, aware that Senior would be furious when he found out that his plans for Orville had floundered so badly.

But, he thought as he watched Orville walk through the outer office past his secretary, Senior really has no cause to be mad at me. Orville quit on his own.

Wild Bill closed the door and went back to his desk, where he said a soft 'Yippee,' and while Orville was sitting at his own desk, drawing two sets of concentric circles on his yellow legal pad, circles with malicious little eyes at the centres, Wild Bill recalled with satisfaction how he had forestalled the FDA investigation of Senior's Special Sauce some years before, saving them both from exposure and disgrace.

And while Orville was drawing huge rabbit ears above the two eyes he had drawn, Wild Bill was thinking. Yes, indeed, this is really a good day for me. That Orville has been nothing but trouble since I hired him, and how he's leaving, and all's well with the world.

48

There was an early July in 1967 when things did not seem to go well with Stan and Fran.

'Well, Fran,' said Stan, incredibly old and crusted by then, to his equally wizened wife. 'Next week our nephew McDonald Crisp will be coming to visit, and I guess we'd better be going into town for supplies again.'

He looked out across his porch and down the slope of the hill, across the purling creek that fizzed with trout and the dirt road that led into Squash, Idaho, then up the opposite slope covered with fir trees where the deer and the antelope gambolled and played, and an occasional herd of elk wandered by in stately splendour. In those woods, hidden from his view and out of ear-shot, crouched the cabin and ten acres he had sold to Senior Hollinday fourteen years before for a goodly profit.

Senior was also due for his annual visit. It seemed that in the past few years Senior and Mac always arrived about the same time; they hunted and fished together in the mountains above the cabin for a couple of weeks each summer, even though both were out of season. Or perhaps *because* they were out of season. It always seemed like a long time before the animals recovered from those visits.

'Goddammit, Stan, we were just in town last week and I just started baking some biscuits. There's no damn reason to go into town today, goddammit. You want to go into town, you go into town yourself or blow it out your ass!'

'No, Fran,' said Stan, thinking about the biscuits hardening in Fran's oven, 'I reckon we'd better go into town today.' Stan never mentioned Fran's language; he had gotten used to the idea that her mouth matched her cooking. 'We got to lay in some liquor for Senior and Mac. You know they like to load up before they go out hunting.'

Stan spat with practised ease from his chair, but his aim was off and he hit the railing. He didn't notice. Above the house the sun slanted down through the green and silver leaves of the quaking aspens and dappled the porch with golden light and silver shade. Stan watched a stag with a magnificent set of antlers stroll out of the woods and down to the creek. He couldn't count the points from his seat, but he could tell it was an old one. Next week they'll probably get him, he thought. If he had had a pipe, he might have been puffing on it with a philosophical air, nodding perhaps over the tenuousness and evanescence of life, the random violence of the universe.

He didn't have a pipe, and in fact he didn't really care much one way or the other about the stag. It was a fine day, and his mind shifted into low gear and laboured up the hill of his intention, which was to get Fran away from those biscuits and into town.

'Come on, Fran, we better get going before the afternoon storms.' A long time passed and Stan waited in the drowsy light, knowing Fran was trying to provoke him. Finally she came out of the house.

'OK, shithead,' she said. 'Let's go.'

The two of them tottered down the slope to their 1951 Hudson coupe, which had once been a deep forest green but was now, after sixteen harsh Idaho winters, an indescribable bile colour. The car started with a long shuddering wheeze, crashed into gear, and rolled reluctantly down the driveway, across the wooden bridge over the creek, and onto the dirt road leading into town. An enormous cloud of dust hovered in the air behind the car, obscuring from view the thick grey clouds piling up in front of the sun.

49

McDonald Crisp, a tall sallow writer with a fast mouth and a dishonest complexion, had started coming out to his Uncle Stan's ranch in 1960, when he was twenty, because he could do there at least a couple of the things he liked to do best: he could get drunk, and he could kill animals. Later, after he had got to know Senior better, he found he could do almost all the other things he liked to do best.

'You know, Hemingway used to go hunting around here,' he

86

told Senior one evening after they had concluded their business together and lay sprawled in two chairs in front of the fire in Senior's hunting lodge, whiskies in their hands.

'Hemingway? Was he that fellow who used to work hay over at the ranch?'

'No. The writer. You're thinking about Mike Hemmings, thin guy with crooked teeth. Had a mean left hook, liked to work in close when he boxed. Saw him knock out Big Swede one summer a few years back at the county fair. It was something. A skinny guy like Mike, dancing around, and suddenly that left hook would lash out. Big Swede fell over like the lights went out. I mean Ernest Hemingway.'

Mac, or 'Big Mac' as he was sometimes called, had once been called 'the new Hemingway' in a review of his first novel, and twice his prose had been described as 'terse'. His first novel was about a man who hunted a killer grizzly with a blackjack and a sharp stick. The *Cleveland Plain Dealer* summarized it as 'a raw, gutsy book . . . Pulse-pounding excitement.' *Women's Wear Daily* raved, 'It describes the heroic journey with precision and verve . . . Sinewy, terse prose.'

Almost four thousand people read the book. Senior was one of the four thousand. Orville was not.

'Good writer?' asked Senior. Things were going very well for him these days. His organization was running smoothly, he was selling more Special Sauce than ever before, and even though the war in south-east Asia was over and the political situation had changed considerably, the import side of the business was continuing without a hitch.

Mac had been doing some work for him for the past eight years, and the rich vein of venality that Senior had spotted in him when they first met was showing no signs of playing out. In fact, Mac had come to depend on Senior more and more.

'The best there is,' said Mac, not really believing that anyone, even Hemingway, was really better than he was. He had improved on Hemingway, in fact. Papa had copped out in the end.

Tomorrow, Mac switched his train of thought, tomorrow the girls will be here. We'll go out and get a buck in the morning, butcher him and hang him to cure in the barn, and in the evening we'll have a party.

Mac knew some starlets and he had all the cocaine he needed and he had just made a great deal of money, and those were three of the other things he liked best. As he stared into the fire his fancy danced with the flames, and the flames were three living starlets licking at his calves in a projector whir and flickering light as over and over he sold the movie rights with fresh deer blood on his hands and in his hair and the thirty-aught-six kicked hard and pleasingly against his shoulder.

Yes, he smiled at the fire, tomorrow the girls will be here.

50

Orville sold his 1968 Ford LTD to an acquaintance who worked in the law offices one floor below Judge Carter's office. He sold his General Electric portable stereo and his Wilson tennis racket. He sold his bed and his easy chair, both of which he had bought second-hand for his otherwise empty apartment. He donated his five grey Robert Hall suits to the Salvation Army. Then one muggy day in late July he packed his small suitcase and prevailed upon a friend to drive him out to the Interstate, where he hitchhiked with a sign, TURNPIKE.

He was picked up by a man from Fairbanks, Alaska, who was driving a 1974 Chevrolet Nova rented from Hertz that morning. He was a salesman for a large drug company who had returned to the home office for a sales meeting. He drove Orville seventeen miles and dropped him off at the Wyandot interchange. He was going to Wyandot to see his sick mother.

In twenty-five minutes Orville was picked up by a 1969 three-quarter-ton heavy-duty Dodge pick-up truck driven by the son of an alfalfa farmer from Wyandot who was going to Chicago to become a factory-trained International Harvester mechanic. He let Orville off at the Munster-Highland interchange after spending four hours and thirty-six minutes detailing for Orville what he had done the night before at the Wyandot Drive-In Theatre with a girl named Marcy. They had watched a double feature of *The Sound of Music* and *The Wild Bunch*. The alfalfa farmer's son proudly told Orville that *The Sound of Music* caused him to lose his virginity.

Orville got a ride almost immediately with a guard at the state prison in Joliet, who drove a 1963 Mercury two-door. He dropped Orville off in Joliet and said, 'Be seeing ya,' as he drove away towards the prison.

He was picked up by a mining engineer in a Mercedes 300SL Gullwing who demonstrated for Orville that it could do one hundred and thirty-five miles an hour on the straightaway. They were finally stopped by a state patrol roadblock near Peru, Illinois. Orville spent the night at the Peru Motor Lodge, where he had dinner in the Machu Picchu Room.

The next morning he caught a ride to Davenport, Iowa, in a 1973 Pontiac Le Mans with seventeen thousand miles on it. The owner, a druggist from Davenport, had been to Chicago for a conference. They talked about the quality of the drugs manufactured by the company the man from Fairbanks, Alaska, worked for. The druggist told Orville they were overpriced.

In Davenport, Orville thumbed a ride with two ladies from Omaha, Nebraska, who had been attending a bridge tournament in Davenport. They were driving a 1973 Oldsmobile Regal 88 convertible. They complained about the mileage all the way to Omaha, where Orville stayed the night in the Omaha Motor Lodge. He had dinner in the Maverick Room.

In the morning he got a ride to Lincoln, Nebraska, in a 1966 Oldsmobile Vistacruiser with white sidewall tyres. In Lincoln, he was picked up by a 1973 Dodge Dart Swinger, pale orange with blue racing stripes, driven by a rakishly dressed pimp from Chicago who was going to Sidney, Nebraska, to visit his sister-in-law, for whom he had some plans. He dropped Orville off in Sydney, where he hitched a ride in a 1969 Buick Skylark with an AM-FM radio. There was nothing on FM, so they listened to the Top 40 from Cheyenne, Wyoming.

It was about this time that Orville started seeing signs beside the road that said LITTLE AMERICA, WORLD'S LARGEST SERVICE STATION, or STOP IN LITTLE AMERICA. GOOD FOOD. LODGING. The signs showed ever-decreasing mileage to Little America.

The Buick dropped Orville in Cheyenne, and he spent the night in the Cheyenne Motor Lodge, where he had dinner in the Mustang Room.

The morning of the fourth day of his journey, Orville got a ride in a 1965 Volkswagon van with over a hundred thousand miles on it. It was driven by two army veterans who talked about Nam, but they didn't know anyone Orville knew.

They stopped for gas at the Li'l Injun station, and Orville

said good-bye. He had four thousand six hundred and fifty dollars in American Express travellers' cheques and one hundred and thirty-two dollars in cash.

He was in Little America.

51

Frank Perkins was travelling back to the base. He had been away for over a month and had raised his score by ten; he carried the ears in his pack as proof.

Someone else might have found the rains oppressive, but to Frank they were a blessing. They muffled sound, kept the enemy confined and the American A-5s and F-111s from flying. There was, among the tangled paths through the abandoned rubber plantations, a wonderful peace, marred only by his tortured thoughts of Muffy Schmidlapp Perkins, who sang lullabies accompanied by a reedy saxophone to his son, Henry. Henry would be almost three now, and Frank was beginning to wonder if little Henry would resemble him. Recently he had begun to have doubts.

He walked steadily through the dripping forest, his eyes moving constantly to both sides, looking for wires, disturbed earth, suspicious regularities, anomalies, traps. Frank had got used to survival.

Through rare breaks in the foliage overhead the clouds seemed close enough to touch. Rain fell steadily, straight down through air that was already saturated, as though it were forming spontaneously at all altitudes and scoring the humid air with vertical lines. Frank jogged through the rain as though he were going through the beaded curtain of a Saigon brothel.

He jogged all day, stopping only twice to eat. He had left the village headman in Cambodia ten days earlier, and then the monsoon started and Frank had moved slowly, alone, through Cambodia, across the Mekong, and into Vietnam. Now he was getting close to Fire Base Franklin. There were signs of American patrols along the trail: gum wrappers, cigarette packs, ration tins, one GI sock, half a shattered helmet liner, a Polaroid photograph of two nude Vietnamese girls trying to look inviting, a packet of used Gillette razor blades. Frank paused once to dismantle a Viet Cong booby trap, and then sat down a few feet off the trail to think.

It was night when he got up again. He slipped quietly away from the trail and threaded his way through the trees towards the base, now only four kilometres to the north-east. The darkness seemed to intensify, and Frank let his eyes rove upwards so his peripheral vision could pick out only the trunks of trees, a darker black against the almost-black of rain and night.

Three kilometres from Fire Base Franklin he crossed another trail, this one leading to the next base up the line. Here he settled down to wait.

He waited four days. On the third day a VC patrol approached and, without detecting Frank, settled in to bide their time. They were waiting for an American to stray down the trail; the next day they were rewarded by Specialist Fourth Class C. D. Mabey, a recently arrived volunteer from Moline, Illinois, who figured that killing gooks (or dinks, he wasn't sure which) might be a lot of fun. He strolled down the path as though he were taking a walk in the rain on the streets of Moline, Illinois. He was blown apart with a suddenness that surprised even Frank.

But before the sound had died away, Frank was nicking his way throug the Viet Cong contingent with a speed that almost matched the attack on SP4 Mabey. The five VC were dead within seven seconds, all with slit throats.

Frank collected the ears and put them in his pack. Then he carefully gathered what was left of SP4 Mabey's effects – dog tags, wallet, name tag from his uniform – and replaced them with his own dog tags, his pack, and his uniform top, which he carefully burned.

He made certain there could be no positive identification of SP4 Mabey through dental patterns or fingerprints, and then he melted away into the rain-filled jungle, leaving behind solid evidence that Lieutenant Perkins had taken five of the bastards with him when he went.

52

'Well!' said Senior after Miss Freemont had ushered Elmo Laurel into his office. His hands were folded on his desk, which was bare except for a blue memo form. Elmo presumed that memo had to do with him. 'Well!' Senior repeated. 'Sit down, sit down.' Senior waved vaguely at the straight-backed chair beside his desk.

'Our Mr Steckbeck feels you're just the man for the job we have in mind here.'

'Mr Steckbeck said you'd tell me what I'll be doing here,' Elmo countered.

'Indeed. Yes, indeed, hmmm,' said Senior, watching Elmo carefully. Elmo sat straight in his chair, his expression properly balanced, he hoped, between enthusiasm and disdain. Senior, a keen judge of character, sized him up as the perfect employee – loyal, competent and unintelligent.

'Well!' said Senior again, after a long silence, the faintest hint of encouragement in his voice, a suggestion that it was Elmo's turn to talk.

Elmo, for his part, thought that he had put a question to Senior and was waiting for a reply. Slowly a tendril of suspicion unfurled in his mind. This man was trying to manipulate him, Elmo Laurel, a man who had served his country faithfully for twenty years. His eyes narrowed slightly and his silence deepened.

'So you've been in the army?' Senior asked at last.

'Retired a few months ago after twenty years. Master sergeant.' Elmo was glad of a question he could answer.

'Mr Steckbeck tells me you're a suspicious person. Not given easily to trust. Like to keep your distance.'

'Well, I don't . . .'

'Mr Steckbeck tells me you're a highly disciplined person, used to taking orders. And giving them.'

'Well, I . . .' Elmo was confused again. Senior's tone seemed to imply disapproval, yet Elmo had understood that he was qualified. Why else was he being interviewed by the president of the company?

While Senior waited for Elmo to formulate his answer, he leaned back and gently fingered a gold ball-point pen taken from the inside breast pocket of his suit jacket.

'Well,' Elmo began, picking his way carefully through the sentence. He sensed danger. 'I was a sergeant in the army. It was my job to obey orders, and to give them. I was good at my job.' His tone was slightly aggrieved.

'Quite right,' said Senior, leaning forward to carefully draw two lines under the word 'paranoid' in the memo on the desk. 'We need a man who can follow orders. And give them.'

Relief flooded through Elmo. He'd given the right answer! 'Yes, sir.'

'I understand you know something about preparing food?'

'Yes, sir. I was a mess sergeant.'

'Good. Good. We need someone who understands foods. What we have in the company here is a department that produces a Sauce.' Sauce was always capitalized when Senior said it. 'This is a very sensitive area with us. Much of the firm's income depends on this department. We are the largest manufacturer of this product in the country. In the world, in fact. There are, as perhaps you know, rivals everywhere, people who would be glad to find out the secret of this product, what makes it so successful.

'We need someone in this department who can help us prevent that from ever happening, someone who will be absolutely loyal to us, who can not be bought off by a competitor. We need a counterespionage agent in the Special Sauce department.'

53

Stan and Fran did all their shopping at the McGuffin General Store in Squash. In a surge of leaden dust they parked their ancient Hudson in front of the store just past the blinking stoplight and opened their doors. Stan crept around the front of the car to Fran and the two of them, leaning into each other, tottered into the store.

'Why, Stan and Fran, how nice to see you of a Friday for a

change.' Miss McGuffin, an indeterminate woman who gave an impression of extreme narrowness – narrow face, narrow shoulders, narrow hips, narrow profile from top to bottom – wavered behind the dry goods counter. Opposite her stood a mottled individual with an air of cunning.

'Blow it out your ass,' Fran muttered under her breath. In fact, she rather liked Miss McGuffin, whose father had founded the McGuffin General Store back before Squash had gotten its second gas station – a Li'l Injun station as it happened, operated by a gentleman everyone felt would be perfect for Miss McGuffin.

There was a rumour, revived on occasion, that he had once proposed to her, but that she had turned him down. He did go into something of a decline not long after he opened the station, and it was never as prosperous as the major oil company's station at the other end of town.

'Stan and Fran,' she introduced them, 'I'd like you to meet Hiram Quint. He's new to these parts, from back East like yourselves. Just got a job out there at that nuclear reactor place. By the way, just what is it you do out there, Hiram?'

'I'm in security maintenance,' Hiram answered, showing an incomplete set of lavender teeth.

'Security maintenance. Hmmm. Well, Hiram, this here is Stan and Fran, who are also from back East, from New Jersey, I think it was, but they've lived out here so long they're practically natives. They own the Hay There Ranch out on County Road Three-fourteen. I imagine their ranch just about borders on the government property where you work, Hiram.'

'I wouldn't know,' Hiram said. 'I just got here.'

'Of course, of course,' said Miss McGuffin, a special note of warmth easing into her voice. If anyone but Stan and Fran had been there, a new rumour would have started right then.

'What part of the East you from?' asked Stan. 'New York?'

'I'm from the, ah, Midwest,' said Hiram. He showed a strange reluctance to talk about it.

'Yes,' said Stan doubtfully.

'What part of the Midwest you from, sonny?' Fran shouted, startling everyone in the store but Stan.

'Just around,' said Hiram with an incomplete gesture. 'You know, big cities. Traffic. Pollution, noise.'

'That why you came out here?' Fran shouted again.

'Uh-huh. Peace and quiet.' Hiram seemed anxious to leave.

94

'You done this kind of work before, sonny?' Fran was even louder.

'You mean security maintenance?'

'Yeah, that's it. Police work?' She screamed, thinking Hiram a bit deaf.

'No,' he said. 'No, I've never done this kind of work before.'

54

'I've never known anyone with a Dodge van before,' said Orville. 'Especially one with a water bed in the back. I used to have a 1958 Ford Edsel convertible, and for a while I had a 1968 Ford LTD. And a few years ago I knew a lawyer with a Nimrod camper. He even went camping with it. Took his kids. And his wife's kids. But I never knew anyone with a van.'

Orville and Bobalou were sitting in the front of the Dodge van. Between them on the console sat two large Cokes in paper cups, a few chips of ice floating on the tarry surfaces, a medium pepperoni and mushroom pizza, two ice-cream sandwiches and a box of Good and Plenty.

They were parked in Row L at the Mustang Ranch Drive-In Theatre, where they had already watched *Castle of Horror* and *The Million-Dollar Duck*. They were waiting for the third feature to start. This was the third night of their fifth month together, and the theatre had just opened for the summer of 1975 – its eighteenth season.

On the screen before them a large clock face showed 'Five Minutes to Show Time.' An animated second hand began to sweep around the face of the clock.

'Orville,' said Bobalou from the driver's seat. She paused to nibble her way up one side of a piece of pepperoni and mushroom pizza and down the other side. She gave Orville the thin strip left from the middle. 'You are sometimes strangely naïve for a man from the East, but you are the teenage dreams of a girl from Long Prairie, Wyoming, come true, and I think I'm going to hang on to you.'

'You know,' said Orville after he'd finished the strip of pizza

95

and watched Bobalou do the same thing to another piece, and eaten the middle again, 'meeting a girl with a 1974 Dodge van was certainly the most wonderful thing that ever happened to me. The fact that that girl was you is especially wonderful and nice and I hope you do hang on to me.'

The screen clock showed, 'Four Minutes to Show Time'. A small cartoon mouse crept out of his cartoon hole in the corner of the screen and looked up at the second hand sweeping around to 'Three Minutes'. The tiny loudspeaker hooked over the window next to Bobalou tootled mouse music. Bobalou chewed her way up and down another wedge of pizza and fed the centre to Orville, watching him with large brown eyes.

'Three Minutes to Show Time' passed.

'Orville,' said Bobalou as she finished the last piece of pizza and handed him his section. 'You have a future in Little America, you know. Chuckie can't run the Li'l Injun station by himself, and it looks like Slim is never going to regain his wits. You could probably settle down here with a share of the station.'

'I like it here, Bobalou,' said Orville. From the speaker a tinny fanfare announced, 'Two Minutes to Show Time.' 'It was always my plan to settle here, in fact, and since I met you I certainly haven't thought of leaving.'

'Orville,' said Bobalou, unwrapping the two ice-cream sandwiches and handing one to Orville, 'I'm very glad you like my van.'

'And I'm glad you like my body,' said Orville, and they laughed as they always did after this exchange. 'One Minute to Show Time' went by.

'Orville,' said Bobalou, finishing her Coke. She put the Good and Plenty in the glove compartment. 'What is the next feature here at the Mustang Ranch Drive-In Theatre?'

'I think it's *Jesus Christ, Superstar*.'

'Orville,' said Bobalou, reaching for him. 'Let's lie this one out.'

The cartoon mouse, which had been watching the clock count down, turning periodically to shrug at the audience, now picked up a bugle from nowhere and introduced 'Show Time' with a flourish and a drumroll, with a tootle and a toot, and Orville was thinking, Now

In the back of the van
The bouncing began.

55

Andrew, thought Flora all those many years later, was magnificent, lifting his shiny nose up into the sunlight to confront that policeman with aplomb and a powerful dignity. Then she and Andrew had veered apart for some weeks of anguish and longing, and she would catch her hand fluttering of its own volition off to the side, as though straining to envelop once again the white hugeness and shine of his organ. She imagined, from time to time, that nose sliding down her groove, as though it were a mighty liner launched at last down the dry-dock stays with champagne and speeches to crash with a rumble of spray into her surging ocean, and she would twitch with unfulfilled longing.

One day Andrew called her. 'The policeman has gone to St Louis, where I understand he has relatives. He will never work in this town again, and perhaps St Louis will be less hospitable than he might think. There are, after all, seventeen Kernel Korn's Drive-In restaurants in the greater St Louis area.'

'Oh, Andrew, are you sure?'

'Quite sure,' Andrew promised her over the phone, and Flora felt the hope that they would not be found out pop into focus in her head. 'Perhaps you might be going shopping sometime soon,' Andrew suggested without pausing for breath. 'Downtown, perhaps, say, this afternoon at three?'

And Flora felt a second hope explode like the Fourth of July and her hand began to stroke the phone receiver.

'I do have a few things to do downtown this afternoon,' she said, and suddenly the idea of spending the rest of her life sewing name tags into Orville's underwear seemed to be less than she should expect from life.

She showered and drove downtown in the same fake Givenchy she'd worn the last time she'd been with Andrew. A haze of golden-brown spring sunshine mellowed the dark brick buildings and tarnished fountain sculptures with the magic of desire.

At three she strolled along the street, window-shopping and glimpsing reflections of herself in sunlight and cream. She met Mr Winkler by accident, and they chatted a while, and then he offered to show her how to get to his office via the freight elevator, and on the way up they didn't see a soul.

'Why, Andrew,' she said as he unlocked the side door to his office and bowed her in. 'A secret entrance!'

'Not secret, Flora, but quite secure,' he said, carefully locking it behind him. 'I don't want to be disturbed,' he said into his intercom. 'I'm working on the Philadelphia contract.'

Then he and Flora lurched towards each other in a thick mist of lust and within seconds were naked on the black leather couch in his black-and-gold-papered presidential private bathroom finishing what they had started so many weeks before in the front seat of his Lincoln Continental.

56

Three weeks after Orville received a high school diploma, he clobbered himself on the head with his mother's Wedgwood lamp. At that time the magic land of Little America was a small flame in his mind, dimming and brightening in the changeable winds of adolescence, but on the whole burning in him as staunchly, and with as much reality, as Oz. That sacred hamburger he'd eaten those years ago when he was nine had seemed at that time, and still seemed in retrospect, to be the Last Supper of a condemned man, before the blade of Camp Tomahawk fell on the neck of his childish freedom.

Little America in those days was, of course, a dusty, tawdry affair, a sloppy stop on a meagre blacktop highway crawling across a little-populated region. But to Orville's nine-year-old eyes it was vast and clean and simple, a place that could give him the room to fumble the ball and be as short as he really was.

When his father was home his clumsiness and size were brought to his attention with a droning constancy that seemed to be a kind of critical Muzak, playing the tunes of his failure over and over.

Still, Orville at sixteen was not entirely sure that Little America was a real place. Perhaps it was, like Oz, a dream. When he told Senior that day in the hospital that he wanted to go there, to have his own gas pump in Little America, Wyoming, he was really firing the first shot (excluding the Wedgwood lamp, which didn't count) in the war with his father that was to rage for the next sixteen years; it was a war that Orville's implacable enemy was never even aware of.

Orville at twenty looked down at his diploma from Harvard and thought that Little America must be at least as real as this; that it had, in fact, a presence on the maps and in that place. He turned to Fred C. Dobbs, standing next to him in his rented black academic gown, and asked, 'How do you feel?'

Fred pursed his bitter mouth. He glanced up at the sky and drew in his breath. He looked around at the pleasant Cambridge spring, the colourful parents smiling and buzzing, the rows of graduates in Accounting and Business and Art and Engineering and Foreign Languages and Geography and History and Journalism and Music and Political Science and Physics and Sociology and Theology and Veterinary Science and Zoology. 'I dunno,' he replied.

'I have here a degree in Accounting with a minor in Russian,' said Orville. 'I will be going to Yale Law School in the fall. I don't know how I feel, either, but I keep thinking about Little America, where I could turn my absence of ambition into an asset.'

'I have a degree in Classics,' said Fred C. Dobbs. 'Do you know what can be done with a degree in Classics? I'll tell you what can be done with a degree in Classics. Nothing. I know a lot about Greek epigraphy. In fact I like Greek epigraphy. It's OK with me.'

'Something will turn up,' said Orville. 'It always does. At least, that's what they say.'

Orville at twenty-five, just out of the army, when all his friends were either Young Republicans or warriors in the underground, small talkative Orville had by then told so many people about Little America that at the end of the long tunnel through the mountain of his father's plans for him he could see the light of that tiny candle first lit when he was nine burning ever more brightly as the realization that the high school diploma, the Harvard diploma, the Yale Law School diploma, the job as law clerk to Wild Bill Carter, nothing, had added one inch to his stature nor given him the ability to catch a softball to his father's satisfaction.

So at last he said 'Why not?' to Little America.

57

'Well, why not?' said Senior to Margot.

It was the second sentence Senior uttered after he stumbled through her front door, and he was heartened that he hadn't said, 'Ny whot?'

'I'll go mix us one,' and she swirled from the room in an aromatic breeze that sent the hairs on the back of Senior's neck quivering outwards like a flight of arrows from the battlements. The fermentation in his groin had flushed away into the swamp of embarrassment and humiliation he had suffered at his verbal fumble.

So when he'd blurted out that he'd like to fuck her phone, Margot's silvery laugh crinkled up his spine like the spiky roller from the inside of a music box, sending a feverish musical sequence of pain and degradation through the sudden void in his abdomen. And when she asked him if he'd like a drink, he wanted nothing more than to erase forever his terrible entrance into this house, to creep back into her flower garden and press himself into the earth beneath her living-room window to be a dreaming zinnia at that tiny gap in her drapes, or better yet a stone in the dark safety of the ground.

And he wanted to flee the house, run back to his car and drive through the night, go to another city and change his name, get a job in a hardware store, live in a roominghouse the rest of his days and forget his terrible secret shame.

Instead, he asked 'Why not?' with casual grace, and arranged himself on the sofa in perfect accord with all his fantasies, his arm draped across the back as though Margot's shoulders were already there and all he need do to feel their creamy texture would be to drop his hand accidentally and have within his grasp all his heart's desire.

Margot came back into the room, placed his drink on the glass-topped coffee table in front of him, and carried hers over to the easy chair oppostie, where she curled her feet beneath herself and cradled the crystal glass between her hands. She watched Senior steadily with her luminous eyes, he felt the shock of paralysis zap through his body, and for an eternity he couldn't move or breathe.

'Uh,' he finally said, reaching for his drink with the arm on the back of the sofa that he suddenly felt was like an extra growth, some kind of goitre that no one would mention out of pity.

'What brings you out this way, Senior?'

'Uh,' said Senior again. He realized that Margot hadn't understood his excuse about the car and he was afraid to try it again, so he drained his drink in one long series of swallows, set it down, and leaned forward with a deeply sincere look on his face.

'I-came-to-see-you,' he blurted out in one resonant spurt.

'Why, Senior, how very thoughtful of you.' Margot's voice was a cool, damp cloth stroking across Senior's brow with the touch of one of the Sisters of Mercy.

'You know Owen's away,' she said in a voice that relit the pilot light of Senior's longing.

'We're here alone,' she said, and the oven in Senior's groin roared into flame and the cake of desire began to rise.

'So I'm really afraid you can't stay here very long,' said Margot, slamming the oven door. The flame went out and the cake collapsed.

58

Elmo was slightly dazed by his interview with Senior. Unable to tell whether he had made a good impression, unable to follow the speed with which his fortunes had seemed to change – first up, then down, and then he was being guided through the maze of vats and pipes in the Special Sauce plant – he felt a cautious mixture of elation and perplexity.

It was warm in the plant, and very humid. At the junctures of the enormous pipes, where they bent in another direction, curls of aromatic steam twisted up from relief valves. The sterile white walls were dulled with condensation. Elmo felt as though he were moving through an absolutely white tropical jungle. Some of the pipes seemed to hold barely contained within them the roar of underground rivers as ingredients compressed by terrific pressures moved from room to room to be weighed and tested and mixed.

Figures dressed entirely in white, with gloves and masks, moved through the blinding gloom in utter silence, the background roar and their paper-soled shoes muffling the sounds of their footsteps.

'We make over eight thousand gallons of Special Sauce every day,' Senior shouted to him over the suck and gurgle of a huge vat, into which the white-frocked and sexless figures were pouring powders and liquids from five-gallon drums.

'What?' shouted Elmo, who thought he hadn't heard right.

'Eight thousand gallons *a day*!'

Elmo edged closer to the vat and peered in. A pimple appeared on the surface and rapidly rose to become an enormous boil that burst with a deep violent burp, followed by a terrible sucking sound as the contents of the vat were vacuumed through a huge drain in the bottom. Within seconds the stainless steel glistened as though it had just been scoured by a battalion of privates on KP. Elmo was impressed. Someone shouted orders and one of the workers turned a wheel, closing the drain, and as Senior led Elmo away more ingredients were being poured into the vat.

In the relative quiet of a connecting corridor, where only the muted roar of the pipes indicated the powers and pressures at work in the Special Sauce plant, Elmo asked Senior how he was to keep tabs on the workers if they were dressed so anonymously, and how he could ever know if any of them were keeping lists of ingredients to sell to another company.

'Oh, no,' said Senior. 'You needn't worry about the people who work in *that* room. Those ingredients there go into everyone's Special Sauce – mayonnaise, cream of tartar, things like that. Anyone could know about that. We have a special ingredient that those workers know nothing about, except that it exists. It's added elsewhere in the plant.

'For now that need not concern you. For the first few weeks, anyway, perhaps you should just sort of mingle with the men, get to know them, how they like their jobs, whether they feel they are making enough money. See if there are any malcontents, union organizers, people like that. You know, troublemakers. Report to me personally in a month or so, when you feel you have a grip on the situation here. We'll give you the title of

'Taste Consultant', so you can move freely about the plant. Feel free to make suggestions about the Sauce at any point along the process. We're always trying to improve the flavour.'

'What about the special ingredient? I can't make suggestions unless I know what it is.'

'No. Don't worry about that either. It's added last, and besides, it has no flavour. It's a kind of preservative.'

59

It took Hiram Quint five years to drift his way from the unemployment lines of St Louis to the subcontracted, fully automated Hollinday Enterprises Methane-Cooled Slow-Burn Breeder Reactor maintained in the plot of ground known as R-2317/A on the aeronautical charts. The breeder reactor was the first of its kind, designed, on an experimental basis, to produce highly toxic, quality plutonium for the Pentagon. Owen wouldn't deny, if he were asked, that his late father's good friend General Richard 'Dick' Carter had a hand in sending the contract his way.

Hiram was hired to be the only known employee of the facility through an employment office in Boise that specialized in what were known in the trade as 'sociological dysjunctives.'

He had changed his name five different times since leaving St Louis on his erratic odyssey across America, until he realized that no one cared any longer what he called himself, and so he went back to his real name. It was the only one he could get used to answering to; he'd found himself getting fired from job after job for failing to respond to orders.

The employment agency knew for a fact that Hiram had left his police job under something of a cloud, and that he had had trouble finding work in St Louis. The agency knew he had changed his name five times and worked at various menial, unpleasant tasks. The employment specialist who interviewed him knew that his teeth were mottled and that he had untrustworthy eyes. He knew that Hiram was only marginally competent at life.

But he also knew that the Hollinday Enterprises Methane-

103

Cooled Slow-Burn Breeder Reactor was fully automated, virtually foolproof, totally secure, completely uninteresting to even the most dedicated foreign agent, and that the last security maintenance officer at the plant had lapsed, after three unrelieved years there, into a strange state of such intense boredom that he had fallen into narcolepsy and died after thirty-seven days of sound sleep. He was found after an indeterminate time by a uranium marshal accompanying the annual routine inspection and Pentagon pick-up crew.

When Hiram drove up to the plant he found the facility surrounded by cyclone fencing topped with barbed wire. He unlocked the gate with the key given him by the employment agency. He drove his 1963 Ford Granada bought with the two-hundred-dollar advance given him when he took the job through the gate and carefully locked it behind him. Then he drove the final three-quarters of a mile to the reactor itself.

'This is it?' said Hiram to himself. He saw a modest government-green cinder-block building perhaps two storeys high with no windows. There was one door, which he parked in front of. The faded pink of the Ford contrasted disconsolately with the building's green. The key to the gate also opened this door.

Inside Hiram found a room with a tiny built-in kitchen, an army cot, a closet with seventeen empty hangers, a battered navy surplus desk and chair, and a 1965 calendar from an insurance company with the first five months missing. On the back wall was a huge, solid steel door that his key did *not* unlock.

'This is it?' Hiram repeated. He went outside and walked around the building. There were no other doors, no windows anywhere, no marks or signs. He heard no sounds but the wind scraping gently through the pines on the hillside behind the plant, bird calls filling the clean mountain air.

It did not occur to Hiram that the air around him was filled with minute invisible particles zipping and waving through the building, his body, the birds and trees at speeds incomprehensible to someone who drove a 1963 Ford Granada. He got into the car and drove into town to buy supplies. There he would meet Stan and Fran and Miss McGuffin.

60

Life in general and business in particular had become considerably simplified for Frank Perkins over the past few years.

First, his death had taken the pressure off him to perform for his country's military. His remains, or rather SP4 Mabey's remains, had been sent home in a plastic bag covered with medals and citations, where it had so upset his twin sister Mary Lou that she up and married the first marine she met, a skinny second lieutenant with large ears who spent the rest of the Vietnam conflict doing what he loved best: he organized and ran the distribution of footwear to a regiment of marines in Opa Locka, Florida.

Mary Lou grew to like Florida.

Second, Frank found that since the end of the American involvement in south-east Asia interference with his business life had dwindled away. He no longer had to juggle his way through an insanely complex edifice of corrupt officials and bureaucratic bribery. He no longer had to worry that his material might be accidentally incinerated in the course of some meaningless jungle battle or bombing mistake. As a result, his profits had risen sharply and his annual work load was reduced to one or two months. The rest of the year he lived with three Cambodian girls in a villa not far from the river. The nature of his business won him the approval of the new national government.

Now he stood beside two Gold Medal flour sacks on a beautiful deserted beach somewhere on the east coast of Vietnam. Golden sand stretched away on both sides of him, curving behind the lush growth at his back. Birds and monkeys chattered and flashed through the green, and above the sun shone brightly. Frank, wearing only a pair of Jantzen swim trunks, glanced at his diver's watch. It was almost time.

The two one-hundred-pound flour sacks were stacked carefully, one atop the other, above the high tide line. The rich blue water slapped gently on the sand with a benignity that was unusual even for this Edenic spot. Frank waded out on the soft sand and swam a few yards. He was deeply tanned.

105

Then he stopped and stood knee-deep in the warm water and looked out to sea. Almost immediately a periscope broke the surface a few hundred yards out, and a submarine rose slowly from the water as it it were on a freight elevator. As it cruised closer to shore at an almost imperceptible speed, Frank could see sailors preparing a rubber raft on deck. The script on the bow of the submarine was Russian.

A bearded man in an officer's uniform guided the raft in to shore, pulling up the motor as the rubber grazed the sand. He climbed out and shook Frank's hand.

'Is all here?' he asked in a thick Slavic accent.

'One hundred kilos,' Frank answered in Russian. 'Just like last year.'

'Da. Good.' The officer realized Frank spoke his language and reverted to it gratefully. He was new on this run. Reaching into the raft, he pulled out an attaché case which he handed to Frank.

Frank opened it and counted its contents. One hundred thousand dollars in gold bullion. One hundred thousand dollars in dollars. One hundred thousand dollars in piastres. One hundred thousand dollars in roubles. One hundred thousand dollars in Swiss francs. Frank removed some roubles and counted them off into the officer's hand. 'That should be correct,' he said.

'Da.' They loaded the two flour sacks into the rubber raft. Frank helped him push off and then watched as the Russian officer motored back to the submarine and loaded the flour sacks and raft aboard. He watched until the submarine cruised to deeper water and disappeared. Then he went for another swim.

61

Senior was in a very bad mood the morning after Bobo Winkler's coming-out party. First his car acted funny, and then Andrew Winkler met him for lunch and it seemed that things were going wrong.

'You do something with the Special Sauce, don't you?' Andrew asked bluntly as he settled down in Senior's lavishly panelled office. He stared at his neatly trimmed fingernails; his hands lay neatly folded in his lap. Only that morning, he had spoken to his host's wife on the phone to tell her about the party and to arrange their next meeting, and he felt a certain smugness.

'We have, as you know, a special ingredient, a kind of preservative that gives the Sauce something other sauces don't have. The special ingredient is a secret.' Senior's voice, singed around the edges with suspicion and hostility, was beginning to smoulder. He stared at Andrew's imposing nose and wondered what Babs Winkler saw in her husband.

'I have an idea,' said Andrew, still looking at his nails. He had had them manicured for the party and to him they looked remarkably elegant. 'That is, I may have an inkling of what the special ingredient is.' His hands were very soft and white. They reminded him of Flora's thighs, so smooth. He tented his hands in front of his face and slowly lowered his nose between them.

'I doubt it,' Senior snapped with a bit more emphasis than he intended. His voice was beginning to curl at the edges with the effort of keeping his mounting anxiety and aggression in check. The Kernel Korn's chain was HIP Inc.'s best customer. 'I mean,' he continued in a more reasonable tone, 'I am the only one who knows what the special ingredient is. Unless you know what to look for, a chemical analysis would be useless.'

'None the less,' said Andrew, whipping his hands away from his nose with a sudden guilty start, 'I have a good idea what it is.'

'Let's go to lunch,' said Senior suddenly, jumping up from behind his desk. Andrew shrugged and followed him out to the parking lot, where Senior viciously backed from his slot, slammed on the brakes, which mysteriously failed, and crashed his dark maroon Coupe de Ville into the rear quarter-panel of Andrew's Kernel Korn's delivery truck.

'Goddam it,' Senior shouted. He got out, slammed the car door, and strode back to his office. Andrew, slightly dazed by the accident, followed him.

'Let's have a drink,' said Senior. He mixed them and called his wife to send Orville out to pick them up. Then he called the garage.

After his first stiff drink he felt better. 'What gives you the idea you know what the special ingredient is?' he asked.

'One of the chefs at our Youngstown restaurant wrote me a letter complaining that they weren't getting enough of the

107

Special Sauce. I investigated and found that they were receiving the normal shipments but that he was eating it all. In fact, that's all he'd been eating. We tried switching him to a rival brand, and he went into a terrible depression. Got the shakes. He was very sick and unhappy until we fed him Hollinday Industrial Pharmaceuticals' Special Sauce. Then he was happy again. Depression gone. No more shakes. But he'd turned into such a lousy cook we had to pension him off. Last week he was arrested for mugging a policeman dressed as an old woman.

'I had a chemical analysis run on it, very discreetly. I told them what I thought they should look for. They reported yesterday. They said the Special Sauce contained minute quantities of an opium derivative. It's no wonder the people who use your Special Sauce on their fast-food products sell so many burgers or whatever. The entire country is becoming addicted.'

Senior made a sound like air slowly leaking from a tyre.

62

Elmo had grown to love the Special Sauce plant. He came in the morning with his lunch pail, which he put in his locker in the dressing-room, put on the sterile gown, the mask and gloves, the soft paper shoes, and thus gowned and masked, he stepped through the heavy airtight double doors to the plant and entered another world. His orange armband identified him as a supervisor.

He spent a month exploring the labyrinth of the plant, checking the numbers painted on the walls with the coded numbers on his floor plan. He grew to love the music of the pipes, the torrents of mayonnaise, the song of finely ground relish, the hum of tartar sauce under pressure. He would move through the steam and condensation of the tunnels and mixing rooms with a feeling of freedom he'd never known before.

At lunch he sat with the other workers in the company cafeteria with its alternately blue and orange plastic tables and talked shop. Elmo learned a number of first names, but no one he could as yet put under suspicion.

On occasion he would pass a sturdy grey door with no knob

on it, only a slot for a heavy-duty electronic lock. KEEP OUT. AUTHORISED PERSONNEL ONLY was painted in orange on the door. Elmo suspected the special ingredient was added beyond that door. He followed the pipes from the final mixing stage to this room, where they bent abruptly into the wall. Past the door at the other end of the passage he found the pipes coming out of the wall and travelling on to the warehouse. There the Special Sauce was pumped automatically into one-gallon and five-gallon plastic tubs and sealed, labelled and shipped.

One day, a week after Senior took Margot to lunch, but a year before he visited her, Elmo was wafting through the Mixing Room, drifting from conversation to conversation, trying to get the feel of the mood of the workers, when he overheard two people talking over the din of the plant and stopped to listen. The steamy air floated wreaths of steam around him, giving a white glare to the room, an atmosphere of a Turkish bath. He was only eavesdropping casually, really watching three men haul a heavy white cloth fire hose over to the stainless steel vat to direct a sluggish stream of mayonnaise into it. He recognized Senior's voice.

'Production,' Senior was saying, 'is up to over eight thousand gallons a day. By nineteen eighty we expect to be producing over twenty thousand gallons a day, with expanding overseas markets. We've even had some feelers from the Russians, and since Nixon went to China there seems to be some possibility that that market may now open to us. Imagine what eight hundred million more customers for the Special Sauce could mean to our sales figures!'

'Son of a bitch,' said the other figure in a tone of admiration.

'Those two markets alone, Russia and China, would mean *one billion people* potentially buying foods with the Special Sauce on them,' Senior continued.

'Son of a bitch,' said the voice again, and Elmo thought to himself. That voice sounds familiar. Where have I heard that voice before?

The two figures moved slowly away from the vat and headed towards the airtight doors of the locker-room. Elmo drifted along behind them like a negative of a shadow, a white and silent shape wavering along the floor and walls.

109

63

While Orville, Eggs and Bobalou were eating dinner on 16 June at the Silver Dollar Café, where they were being served by that same Florence Biedernick who over a year before had been propositioned by a man driving a 1973 Cadillac Coupe de Ville, Orville was day-dreaming about the bomb he was making, his ultimate Senior bomb.

As Eggs and Bobalou discussed the specialities on the dessert menu, which included such favourites as Uncle Tom's Cabin Cake and a St Valentine's Day Massacre (a sundae of spumoni with cherry topping), he was mentally designing a bomb about the size of a football that would fit nicely under the spare tyre in the trunk of Senior's 1976 Coupe de Ville. Senior would be by next week on his way to Idaho, and Orville would plant the bomb while servicing the car. Senior had taken some delight, it appeared, the previous year in having Orville service his car, and Orville counted on that same delight this year.

'You're a uranium marshal, Eggs. If you were planning to make a home-made nuclear device, how would you go about it?' Orville vocalized his thoughts.

'You mean hypothetically?'

'Yes.'

'Well, you're a uranium marshal yourself, now, Orv, so I think you know how easy it would be, really. Collect your materials first, uranium hexaflouride or uranium oxide or uranium metal or plutonium or any of half a dozen other readily available substances. Process it a bit, clean it up. Design a timing device from materials you could buy at any local Radio Shack. Get some kind of high explosive to trigger it, some steel as a reflector. Bolt it together. Send three dollars to the National Technical Information Service for the critical-mass summaries. *The Heavy Metals Handbook*, that's the same book we used in the army. Better yet, join the army and become an Atomic Weapons Technology specialist, like we did. It's so simple, even Sergeant Laurel could have explained it. Maybe even done it.' Eggs laughed and sank his spoon into the Whisky Rebellion

Pound Cake Florence had just deposited in front of him. It had whisky in it.

'I'll tell you the truth,' Eggs added in a serious tone, putting down his spoon. 'I belong, or rather belonged, to an organization dedicated to removing Richard Nixon from office. When he removed himself, we had nothing real left to do, so we looked around.'

'What was your organization called?' asked Bobalou. She had forgotten about her dish of plain vanilla ice-cream, which was now called a Valley Forge. The Valley Forge slowly melted, as if spring were coming to the Revolutionary army.

'We called it the Committee for the Liberation of Intelligent Things. We were for sexual liberation, freeing all political prisoners, jobs for everyone, national medical insurance, and removing Richard Nixon – mainly the last. At one time we were thinking of kidnapping Henry Kissinger and bombing the Capitol heating system, but the FBI thought of it first and arrested a bunch of other people; we never could figure that one out. After Nixon resigned we decided to steal nuclear materials so they couldn't be used for military purposes. We were going to dispose of them; awfully idealistic, we were. But the whole organization sort of fell apart, so we disbanded CLIT. It all seemed to be pointless.'

'So I became a uranium marshal. Next best thing, I suppose.'

'Wow,' said Bobalou. 'I sure do like the name, real classy. But what made you give it all up?'

'Two reasons,' said Eggs. 'First, there's so much of the stuff around; they make it faster than we could have stolen and disposed of it. And second, it was no fun, really. The stuff is far too easy to steal.'

64

As the Russian submarine *Prazdnik* stole at silent running through the Arctic waters towards the coast of British Columbia and the Hokai Pass, Captain Grigory Schmidlov counted the roubles on the table before him again. He reflected for the hundredth time on how little of this money was required to maintain the co-operation of the three officers sitting in the ward-room with him; then he counted out the three piles of new bills. He had just finished when the phone next to him chimed softly.

'Yes?'

'We are there, captain.'

'We'll be right up.'

The light on the bridge was dim and red, punctuated by the winking of telltales and cathode-ray screens, radar, and the soft pinging of sonar. The submarine moved almost idly through the water, as though drifting with the tides and currents. Grigory guided it through the Hokai Pass and then turned southward towards the Hardy Inlet.

Fifty metres offshore the sub surfaced and came to a dead stop, and the only sound for a few moments was the whisper of the ventilation system. Captain Schmidlov let out a long breath. 'I will take it in myself,' he said to the officer standing next to him. Everyone moved quietly, as though in a hospital or library, their actions slow and deliberate in the red light.

'Captain?'

'Yes.'

'A ship is approaching. A steamer, perhaps.'

'Must be the regular steamer through the Fitzhugh Channel. We will wait.'

Silence fell again. At last the steamer had passed in the darkness and the sound of her screws faded away. Captain Schmidlov climbed the ladder and had the two hundred-pound sacks of Gold Medal flour handed up to him. He undogged the hatch and climbed out into the cold, late winter air. It was overcast, and small, light flakes of snow floated sporadically into the black water. Grigory could not see the shore, but after checking the compass in his hand he aimed his flashlight towards the east and rapidly turned it on and off three times. He waited a minute and repeated the signal.

Nothing happened.

Ten minutes later Captain Schmidlov began to worry. The sub was deep inside Canadian territorial waters on a mission that was illegal according to the laws of every land Captain Schmidlov had anything to do with, including his own. He had only one hour to complete his mission, and already a quarter of that time had passed without his signal being answered. This was his first such mission; the previous submarine commander, a cousin of his, had retired.

He repeated the signal again, and this time an answering light winked from the shore.

Grigory slid the inflated rubber raft off the deck into the water. Carefully he loaded the two sacks into it and stepped down. Using the oars in the raft rather than the motor, he paddled the raft to shore as silently as possible. This was supposed to be a deserted section of coastline, but one could never be sure. It took almost five minutes to cross the fifty metres to shore, but at last the rubber scraped on the gravel coast and bumped to a halt. A figure swaddled in a heavy parka snapped on a red-shaded flashlight. The red light moved, illuminating the sled dogs and hard-packed snow at the high tide line.

'Help me load it on the sled,' McDonald Crisp's nasal voice came from behind the light.

'Yes. I help you,' offered Captain Schmidlov in his heavily accented English. The two of them quickly loaded the sled. Mac mushed off without a backward look, and Grigory paddled back to the submarine. He was glad to get away.

65

Miss McGuffin, that fevered dream of a Cubist god, all angles and elbows, radiated such a warmth towards Hiram Quint almost as soon as she met him that he felt a fear he had never felt in all his years of police work, so at first he was relieved when Stan and Fran tottered into the store and dimmed some of the radiant hunger Miss McGuffin was putting out.

But Fran's keen questioning soon made him nervous again, and he sidled out of the store, leaving behind the thin lavender trail of his breath dissipating in the air.

'We'll have a case of Old Yardbird whisky, Miss McGuffin,' said Stan after Hiram left. Old Yardbird was what Senior and Mac liked to drink. 'And we'll have our usual order of foods, and Fran needs another flannel nightgown.'

While Miss McGuffin collected their order, Stan and Fran stood there in the store swaying and creaking like the trees at night around the Hay There Ranch house, not saying a word. Miss McGuffin loaded the case of whisky and the food into the back seat of the ancient Hudson and went back into the store, where she picked up her copy of *The Jesus Connection* and tried to continue reading, but her thoughts wandered. Hiram's narrow, cunning face kept drifting up from the page.

Stan and Fran tottered back out to the car and with a fit and a start shuddered off into the deepening gloom of the clouded afternoon. The threat of rain or hail leaned heavily on the humid Idaho air.

They left the paved blacktop highway and turned on to the gravel of County Road 314, where the Hudson began to sway with a rhythmic bounce that started some secret spring of juices moving through Fran's rusted lusts, and she began to squirm on the high upholstered seat of the Hudson in a way that sent the springs under her sproinging into her mellowing centre.

She gradually bounced her way across the seat, and by the time Stan was about to turn off County Road 314 on to the nameless dirt road leading to the Hay There Ranch, Fran had plunged her boney livered hand into the voluminous folds of Stan's trousers and said, 'Stan, I'm a hungry fucker and I want to do it now!'

'You want to do it now, do you Fran,' said Stan, looking down solemnly as Fran's hand crawled through the layers of his stomach in quest of the grail she knew was there. He had no question in his voice when he said it, and his head nodded up and down with the bouncing of the car as it slowed to a stop. Stan forgot to put in the clutch, and the car jerked four times as third gear lugged and burped and the engine stalled.

Fran hiked her flowered skirt up her ancient dumpling legs and popped the buttons on Stan's plaid lumberjack shirt. She tugged at the ornate cowboy buckle carved in silver bas-relief in the shape of Buffalo Bill slaughtering buffalo from a train, and as the first gelid plops of June hail flattened themselves on the Hudson's windshield, Stan's pants were squirmed down his puckered shanks, exposing a pair of enormous polka-dotted undershorts.

Fran's flowered dress, the flowers tiny and orange on the mildewed black background, hooked itself on either side of her iliac crests.

And now, with Stan's rutting urge aroused, Fran's dusty bloomers were rent and disappeared and the hail began to bang on the metal roof. As Stan steered his mighty tanker into Fran's dredged and waiting harbour, the thunder growled around the car as though some primeval god of Hackensack were making it as well.

'Oh, Stan, you fucking fucker,' shouted Fran in a joyous frenzy of juices. 'We're doing it! Oh, boy! Oh, twenty-three skidoo!'

Stan steered his final lengths into the safe exacting harbour of a double, mutual, sockeroo zapping turbulent orgasm, the best in twenty years, not counting the time Stan fell off the bridge into the creek and Fran had fluttered down on top of him like a tent full of feathers to make him warm, and as they came together to the sound of bells and thunder, a megavolted bolt of jagged lightning blasted the 1951 Hudson coupe to melted slag, igniting the case of Old Yardbird whisky in the back and the gas tank, incinerating Stan and Fran on the spot in eternal wedded bliss, and also thereby insuring that McDonald Crisp would inherit the Hay There Ranch in time for the summer hunting.

66

'Well, Margot,' said Senior after his natural ruddy colour had once again risen into his face with the agonizing slowness of mercury in an oral thermometer. 'I guess I'd better go.'

Margot took a contemplative sip from her drink, her feet still curled underneath her on the sea-green easy chair. She had told him he couldn't stay. Resigned, he straightened his tie and gathered the overcooked spaghetti of his muscles into a feeble, stringy preparation for departure.

'Perhaps, Senior, we could have lunch again some time. Like we did last year.' Her large brown eyes rotated towards him like opening night and enveloped him in a shining fog of soft amber Hollywood light, pinning him to the couch, and he slid into soft focus; he saw through the dazzle, through the gauze scrim of his once again renewed hope, those eyes floating in a glycerine bath, bright highlights winking: M-A-R-L-E-N-E D-I-E-T-R-I-C-H.

'I'd like that, Margot,' said Senior. His voice sounded to him like a small reed whistling in very thin air.

'Owen and I are, well, we spend less time together than we used to,' said Margot.

'I'm sure you have plenty of friends. People who would be glad to, er, keep you company,' said Senior, who thought his voice sounded like Donald Duck, a squeaky quack.

'Well, of course,' Margot said, her eyes still radiating a special golden warmth on to Senior's baffled epidermis, which had begun to oscillate wildly between chills and fever, between pernicious nightmare sweat-damp and the dry lizard-leather of a desert toad on a hot rock.

Senior might have been less confused if he had known that at almost that very moment Owen's piston was driving deaf-mute Juanita's engine round and round at a hundred rpm. He might have felt that nothing, in light of that knowledge, would stop Margot from testing out *his* piston on the racetrack of their mutual desire. He might have felt that.

But Senior would have been wrong. Margot was not in the least interested in what Owen might be doing, and had they known about it, it would have done Senior no good whatsoever. Margot sat in her chair, sipped her drink and looked at Senior, and what she saw was the curling slightly grey hair and balding head and sturdy masculine glasses reflecting back to her the luxuriant adoration she knew was everywhere around her in the air. She saw desire, and running always through the finely woven network of her semi-conscious narcissism were the rapid calculations that constantly tallied and adjusted her postures in the world. A fraction of an inch downward tilt to her head, and a lock of chestnut curls fell across her ear; Senior's pulse automatically responded by notching up to ninety. A short swivel of her head to the left, revealing a slightly different view of her cameo profile, and Senior felt an adolescent implosion in his abdomen. Every one of Margot's cells *knows*.

'Lunch,' he croaked. 'Tomorrow?'

'Oh, that would be lovely,' she said as she leaned forward to put her drink on the coffee table, and Senior imagined wonders pillowing forward in her blouse.

'Perhaps we could see a bit more of each other, Senior. You really are an attractive man,' she said, and Senior, who was at the same time leaning forward as well to pick up his already empty drinks, continued to fall forward into her opening blouse, smacking his forehead smartly on the glass-topped coffee table.

67

Senior and Andrew had come to an agreement that Christmas Eve so long ago after Bobo's coming-out party.

It seemed that Andrew was a very shrewd operator and had indeed discovered the secret of the Special Sauce. Since then he got a tour of the plant every year in the early spring. He received as well exclusive rights to the doctored Special Sauce in any area that had, or would have, a Kernel Korn's Drive-In Restaurant; as a result Kernel Korn's outsold all other fastfood outlets more than two to one. A high percentage of that was repeat business. Regulars at Kernel Korn's stayed regular.

Nineteen seventy-four was no exception to the agreement for the annual tour, and Andrew and Senior were so deep in conversation that they didn't notice Elmo stealing along behind them through the steamy glare of the Mixing Room.

Andrew was laughing. 'Son of a bitch,' he said for the third time before they left the room. Senior had mentioned that only the two of them knew what the special ingredient was and how it was put into the Sauce. Andrew found it hard to believe that Senior could be so secure.

'Surely someone else knows what it is?' he asked.

'No,' Senior answered. Elmo hung back, waiting for the door lock to cycle again before going through himself.

'You mean you put the "ingredient" in yourself?' Andrew had a comic vision of Senior pouring huge sacks of opium into the feed mechanism in the locked room. As they stood inside the air lock between the double doors waiting for the air to recycle through the air-conditioners, Andrew was thinking that their agreement did not include poaching rights on Senior's preserve. Andrew and Flora had been meeting twice a month for the past twelve years, and their interest in each other showed no signs of cooling.

Finally the door to the dressing-room swung open and the two men started to strip off their gowns and masks, chatting idly. They didn't notice, a few minutes later when the door opened again, a white-clad figure walking to a locker around the corner. Distantly Andrew registered the sound of a locker door opening, but their conversation was innocuous, so it didn't seem important.

'You got the cheque all right?' asked Senior, taking his suit jacket from the locker and putting it on.

'Oh, yes,' said Andrew. 'It came right on time.'

Senior was paying Andrew a small rebate on the Special Sauce sales, just to defray any inconvenience Andrew might have to undergo should another of his chefs run into a problem with the Sauce. Senior had treated the first one to an expensive clinic, and when he'd been threatened by an investigation from the FDA, he started paying this token rebate to Andrew. Andrew had pointed out to him, back then in 1966, that it would be important for HIP Inc. to maintain a low profile to the FDA, and Senior had concurred.

Elmo appeared around the corner. 'Oh, hello, Mr Hollinday,' he said, feigning surprise. 'I seem to have lost a cuff link. Have either of you seen a cuff link?'

'No,' said Senior. 'I haven't seen any cuff links. Have you seen a cuff link, Andrew?'

'I haven't seen any cuff links out here,' said Andrew, and in Elmo's mental theatre there rose a vision of the country club eight years before, when he saw someone furtively priming this gentleman's pump in the downstairs dining-room, and that someone was none other than his boss's wife, whom Elmo had seen only the day before yesterday walking across the executive parking lot on one of her rare visits to her husband's office.

'Son of a bitch,' Elmo said very softly under his breath.

68

Slim Piggot, his arm forever stiff, stood in the darkness beside the Li'l Injun station in the cricket-laden late June, his eyes fixed as always on a horizon no one else could see. His memory had swirled down the drain the year before when he had swung at his beloved Juanita and missed, and he had used up every aggressive emotion with that swing. He would continue to stand there until some stimulus prompted him to move.

What he could have seen, looking out from the shadowed pool surrounded by the glare from the rotating neon Li'l Injun that revolved in front of the station like an everlasting testimony to the ingenuity of all those Europeans who brought civilization to North America, was the silhouetted figure of Orville Hollinday carefully opening the back door of his cousin's truck. Once again Owen was experiencing the wonders of Juanita's Airstream hospitality, and she had sent the now-docile Slim out into the night, for this was an experience that took her breath away as well.

Orville figured the canisters he was removing from Owen's truck would complete his plan for Senior's car. And when his father drove through Little America in a couple of days, he could plant his evil mushroom in the trunk and all his years of harboured hatred would evaporate in purple flickering smoke.

So he removed the canisters from the back and carefully unloaded them on to the mechanic's dolly beside him. Two, he decided, would do the job. He replaced the now-empty birdcages with canisters filled with sand and put them back into the truck.

The import of what Slim saw was percolating very slowly down through the miasma of his brain. That was his boss and buddy out there working on the truck. Perhaps he ought to help? Slim imagined doors opening in the night on to darkened rooms, rooms filled with primitive unformed fish that screamed and procreated in utter black until the water in the rooms was a suffocating mass of scales and slime.

Slim saw Orville working, and somewhere in the dimness his father bent to the carpet, pointing out for Slim in an angry voice the little messes Slim's pet dog had made; he slogged in sloppy galoshes through a swamp that steamed and gurgled over the tops of his boots and between his toes, a swamp that somehow became Juanita's soft envelope of flesh into which Slim slipped every night, to be mailed in silence through his vague unfocused time-warp into a sleep as dreamless and vague as his waking.

Slim saw Orville carefully close the back doors of the truck and seemed to hear somewhere far away the sound of a door slamming shut with a reverberation that cascaded through both sound and vision. All around him doors closed, shutting him out: his father closed the door, his doggie closed the door,

Juanita closed the door, and behind the door the room filled rapidly with water and screaming fish with enormous jaws and vicious teeth.

Slim whimpered to himself and suddenly at his ear Eggs Freebnik's voice asked, 'Well, look at that! What's old Orville up to there?'

Slim spun around in a slow-motion haze of surprise and fantasy, of rotating neon light and confused loyalty, of pooled shadows filled with accusing eyes, and his bent, rigid elbow swung with him in an arc precisely defined to connect with Eggs's chin, thereby concluding in delayed follow-through the blow he had aimed at Juanita the year before.

69

When Andrew Winkler left the HIP Inc. plant, Elmo's thoughtful eyes followed him out the door and down to his car. They watched him get into his 1974 Lincoln Continental Mark IV and drive away into the brightening spring haze. Then Elmo turned back and walked slowly into the locker-room.

Andrew drove straight to his office, where he called Flora.

'I know this isn't our regular day,' he said with a smile Flora could hear through the phone and her lower abdomen. 'But I was wondering if you might not have a little shopping to do.'

There was a short pause in which Flora could hear the breath roaring rapidly in and out of Andrew's terrific nose; her own breathing sped up to match his. Parts of her body felt so loose, and other parts felt so tight, that she could barely answer him. 'I do have a little shopping to do,' she said at last, thus keeping up the elaborate code they had worked out over the past twelve years. She giggled slightly.

She had thickened only a bit into her forty-eighth year, and Andrew also had thickened some and balded some more. But she still slipped her private key into the separate executive entrance to Andrew's office with a delicious shudder and slid inside, thinking always of the nose that still mounted her thighs with a magic that never faded.

He was standing in the bathroom in front of the full-length

mirror looking down at his quivering erection, and when Flora noticed it she gave a little gasp and started tearing at her dress. 'Oh, my God, Andrew,' she said, hopping towards him in a furious cartwheel of flying underwear, trying to get rid of her lemon yellow panties and get her hands on Andrew's ivory shaft at the same time. Finally, her clothes scattered like wreckage around her, she dropped to her knees and cupped his terrible heat in her two soft, sensitive hands. She gave it a kiss or two before Andrew lifted her to her feet and led her to the leather couch, where he sat her down and put himself into the position of nasal advancement. Her knees started shaking uncontrollably as Andrew notched his nose between them and crawled its boney ridge and fleshy tip up her inner thigh.

'Oh, my God, Andrew,' she repeated as his hands slid up her legs towards her hips. 'I can't *stand* it!' she said, flinging herself to the deep pile of the black-and-white-patterned shag carpet, knocking Andrew over on to his back and slopping her zinging groin on to his upthrust nose, and at the same time hungrily seizing his hard-on with both hands and stuffing it into her mouth.

'Ohmm mghy Ghhd, Ndrew,' she mumbled with her mouth full, and just then the phone rang.

'Gaaahh!' said Andrew. 'Never mind.' His nose buried itself deeper into her seething centre.

'Mr Winkler,' his secretary's voice piped through the office intercom, 'this gentleman says his call is very important. He is most insistent.'

Andrew struggled to his feet, Flora still clutching and gobbling at his crotch, and picked up the wall phone. 'Yes,' he said, holding his breath.

'Ah, Mr Winkler. Yes, I'd like to meet with you to discuss an evening some eight years ago in the downstairs dining-room at the country club. You were with a Mrs Hollinday at the time. Do you by any chance remember that evening?'

70

Orville and Bobalou had an evening *they* would never forget on the very last day of 1975, when they rented the X-rated room

121

at Little America's newest Sleepy Time Motel. This room, with its red-flocked wallpaper and mirrors, its water bed bigger and bouncier than the one in the back of Bobalou's Dodge van, with a fur spread that felt softer and realer than the one on Bobalou's water bed, this room had a circular bathtub big enough for two and Orville and Bobalou filled it to the brim with bubble bath and settled in to music and champagne imported all the way from California.

'Bobalou,' said Orville, lifting his soapy hand from the water to raise the crystal champagne glass to Bobalou, whose feet wound themselves through the bubbles to snuggle under Orville's ribs. 'Bobalou, I would like to drink a toast to us in this new year that is just coming up. I would drink to the 1974 Dodge van in which we have travelled so far and in so very few miles. May we continue to go nowhere in that Dodge van except maybe all of Little, and maybe all of big America too, and perhaps the world as well. Outer space, Bobalou. All the places we've been. Because I think I love you.'

'Orville,' Bobalou responded, touching the crystal rim of her glass to his with a pure high G of exploding bubbles in it, a tone of alchemical quintessence of both their lives at that very moment. The tone died away, but the smell and sound of bubbles of both bath and wine continued into the perfect evening.

'I love you,' said Bobalou, and she lowered the glass to her perfect lips and drank enough champagne to bring her teeth and tongue into popping life. Then they lay back in the warm water and stared into each other's dreams for a time that was long and seemed short, or was short and seemed long, they were never sure which, and their legs and toes were entangled there.

Finally Orville said, 'Bobalou, I am making my last bomb. This time surely Senior will know in his last nuclear moment the shame and humiliation he's made of my life before he and his Cadillac become an Idaho landmark. I've bombed him before and he's never even noticed. This time he'll notice.' Orville's head lay on the edge of the circular tub and his eyes rested on their mirrored images in the ceiling: Bobalou's face across from his, her breasts and knees and toes, the flower of his manhood and his knees and toes all mixed and mingled in the suds.

'You don't really want to kill your father.' She had neither reproof nor question in her voice, only simple fact.

And Orville really thought in that moment that she was

122

wrong, but he said nothing more and the silence grew and floated with them in the room. Outside, time ticked on towards 1976, but inside, they and their reflections in the ceiling and the quiet that shared them both did not move in time at all. It was as if the crystal chime of the champagne glasses somehow still echoed in their breathing.

At last they woke together from eternity and Bobalou said lazily. 'What's on for tonight?'

'Well,' said Orville, 'in the other room in front of the big round water bed with what feels like real fur on it but isn't is a huge twenty-four-inch television set, and a quick glance at the programmes provided by the Sleepy Time Motel tells me we can watch an outstanding array of erotic delights. For instance, perhaps a production called *Teachers Pet*, with no apostrophe, would be to your liking. Or *The Blue Balls of Scotland*, with real kilts...'

'Oh, Orville,' said Bobalou, smiling.

'We might,' Orville went on, 'stimulate our jaded appetites with a story of sailors on shore leave called *Blow the Man Down*. Or *Ice Cream for Sex* on Channel Sixty-nine. A clever little pun there. But I see by my watch,' said Orville, 'that it is going on to ten o'clock in the world of men, which means that in far-off New York City the crowds at Times Square are beginning to count it down to midnight.'

So Orville and Bobalou went into the other room and lay down together on the almost-real fur rug and watched Guy Lombardo and his heirs play the sweetest music this side of heaven and 'Auld Lang Syne' the new year in around the world hour by hour, and they held each other close and kissed each chaste sweet midnight across America.

71

'Eggs!' said Orville, holding up his friend's left eyelid with his thumb. All he could see was an almond-shaped sliver of white under there. 'Eggs, are you all right?' Eggs gave a long shuddering sigh and tried to wake up.

'Gosh, Orville. I sure didn't mean to hit him like that,' said

Slim hesitantly. 'He said something right behind me and I got scared.'

'Never mind, Slim,' said Orville. 'Just help me carry him into the office and then you mind the pumps for a while, OK?'

'All right, Orville. Whatever you say.' Slim shrugged and lifted Eggs's right arm with his good left hand. Together they half-carried, half-dragged Eggs's still unconscious form into the office. Then Slim shuffled out to the pumps, his bad arm still crooked in front of him, and stood impassively by the rack of oil waiting for a customer.

'Eggs!' said Orville, getting worried now.

'Huh? What happened? Where am I?' His eyes snapped open and he stared for a moment into Orville's worried face. 'Oh, shit,' he said. 'They always say that, don't they. Never mind, I know what happened. That was Slim?'

'That was Slim,' said Orville. 'You startled him. What were you doing back there?'

'Well, Orville, to tell the truth, I was watching you, and it certainly appeared to me that you were stealing some fissionable materials from that truck that has your name on it – Hollinday Enterprises. Are you in the atomic business too?'

'No. That's my cousin's truck. I was, ah, just doing a little security checking. After all, I'm a uranium marshal now myself, and it's my job to see how well things are secured in transporting fissionables. Isn't it?'

'Yes, it is your business, Orville. But you can't shuck me, you weren't just checking the lock on the truck. You were unloading U-235 from the birdcages in there. I saw you.'

Orville wasn't sure of the tone in Eggs's voice. 'Are you accusing me of stealing?' he asked.

'No, Orville, I'm not accusing you. I'm congratulating you. You would have been a hot prospect to recruit into CLIT. Too bad it doesn't exist anymore. Tell me, what are you going to do with it?'

'Well,' said Orville, 'I'm putting together a very small, very clean tactical weapon. Just enough to take care of Dad and his Coupe de Ville. That's what I'm doing with it. He'll be out there in the absolutely deserted wilds of Idaho, all by himself, and he'll explode.'

'I heisted a bit from cousin Owen last year as well, and with this bit here I have enough, I think. When he shows up in a couple of days, well, I'll put the bomb in his car and pack him

124

off to his hunting lodge, where he shoots large animals out of season, and that'll be it.'

'I'll be damned.' Eggs laughed. 'So that's it. You're finally going to carry it through. But what about your cousin Owen. Won't he get in trouble?'

'Well, Eggs, I don't much like cousin Owen; haven't since he gave me a bloody nose in the fourth grade . . .' Orville remembered a sleek, good-looking Owen punching pudgy Orville in his nine-year-old nose and smiled. 'He owns the company and I suppose he can cover for himself, but I don't really think anyone will find out. I replaced the canisters, and besides, I never heard anything about the uranium I stole last year.'

From the pumps an angry voice roared into the Li'l Injun office: 'Goddammit, look what you've done. Jesus Christ!'

Orville rushed out of the office.

Slim was standing vacantly beside a pump, the premium hose in his left hand. The nozzle was pointed at the hole of the gas tank in the customer's car but had failed to connect. The hose was spurting hi-test gasoline all over the left rear fender and trunk lid of Senior Hollinday's brand-new silver Cadillac Coupe de Ville.

72

Senior was not quite knocked unconscious by his pitch on to Margot's glass-topped coffee table, but somewhere close to his ears an enormous Chinese gong was clobbered by a Mr Universe contestant from Muscle Beach, and Senior's eyes rolled up and crossed, looking at Margot through golden waves of deep pain that rose and receded and slowly faded away. Even after the sound had disappeared Senior felt his right eye staring at Margot's right ear, his left eye crossed over to look at her left ear.

He was surprised to find, after a moment, that she was still sitting there across from him, cupped in the foamy sea-green easy chair, looking at him with an expression in which he could read almost everything but concern.

'Senior, are you all right?' she asked. She was relieved that the coffee table had suffered no damage.

125

'Uh, well, uh, yes,' said Senior leaping to his feet as though he had suddenly remembered an appointment. His right knee caught under the edge of the coffee table, lifting it twenty-seven inches off the floor, so that it teetered precariously for a moment. His drink slid down the slick glass surface and dropped the short distance to the deep-pile carpet, scattering four small almost-melted ice cubes in a neat semi-circle. Then Senior straightend his knee and the table dropped back to an upright position.

Instantly he was on his knees, sweeping the tiny cubes back into his glass with his fingers. 'Oh, my God, I'm sorry,' he said, setting the glass carefully on the table again and rising warily to his feet.

'Oh, Senior, really!' said Margot, with the faintest hint of exasperation quavering behind the velvet arras of her voice. 'It's only water by now.'

'Well, I suppose I'd better be going,' said Senior, hoping it wasn't so. His head began to throb, conga drum and castanets to a Latin beat.

'Yes, I suppose you had, Senior, before you really break something,' said Margot. Senior wasn't sure whether she meant break something of *hers* or something of *his*.

She levitated to her feet in a sweet whisper of clothes and gracefully crossed the space between them, her feet not seeming to move at all, and Senior saw only everything he ever wanted coming towards him.

She took his arm and led him firmly towards the front door, still and always the last place Senior wanted to go. He felt a peculiar paralysis seize the arm she held, and his head pounded all the way to her vestibule, where she swung him around and looked deep into his masculine glasses, which had miraculously escaped injury from his fall into the coffee table, though they were perhaps embedded just a tiny bit deeper into the bridge of his nose.

It seemed that the heat of her eyes was fogging up his glasses, and he fell through them into her face and found himself kissing her in a strange way that could have reminded him of the word 'masher' in that infinitesimal moment when their teeth clicked.

'Oh, Senior,' she murmured, and in her head her handsome daddy danced her through a magnolia-heavy night while somewhere in the background an orchestra played Stephen Foster

126

under the full golden moon. Senior stood there with his lips glued, his head throbbing and his fires roaring, and Margot swivelled her vast undulant pelvis forward into Senior's hardening resolve and danced in aching adolescent abandon with her wonderful loving dad.

73

Miss McGuffin's father, a man as narrow in mind as his daughter was in body, had spun three times around a pothole in the state highway to Boise in the winter of 1958 and died, leaving the store to Miss McGuffin, who for nine years more had hungered. She had hungered first for the stranger who opened the Li'l Injun station in Squash, and when that didn't work out she had just hungered.

The stranger had not, in fact, as everyone supposed, actually proposed to Miss McGuffin. He had propositioned her and she had proposed. He turned her down. She tried to explain to him, in her blush-raddled way, that proposals and propositions were not quite the same thing, but he stormed off sullenly to decay at his station in a boozy silence, and over the intervening years the distinction that had once seemed so important to her also decayed.

So when Hiram Quint appeared in her store that fateful day (fateful to Stan and Fran in one fatal way, and fateful to Miss McGuffin in another), he entered like a Limburger miracle from the gods of cheese, and Miss McGuffin was quite prepared by then to ignore the formalities of church and state to fulfill herself and feed that growing hunger. And even though Hiram had sidled out of the store that day, Miss McGuffin kept her sharp eyes on him all the time, knowing that since she had the only store in town he had to come back.

It was two weeks after they buried Stan and Fran, still fused, now and forever, into the melted shell of their 1951 Hudson coupe, a classic car transmuted by nature into what, in a museum setting, might then have been hailed as a milestone of twentieth-century art, a poignant comment on the perils of

127

technological development and the infantile overdependence of Americans on their automobiles, that Hiram returned to the store.

Hiram sidled into the store, leaving behind him the lavender trail of breath that caused honest citizens to stagger when they crossed his wake, and mumbled an order for supplies to a Miss McGuffin who appeared to have twice as many bones as the ordinary human skeleton. So enraptured was she by his entrance that she noticed neither his odour nor the curious lichen on his teeth.

'Certainly, Hiram. I may call you Hiram, mayn't I?' she asked him, feeling a thin electric crackle snap into being from her knee to her crotch, as though her femurs were high-tension lines in danger of overload.

'Yeah,' Hiram replied, a white crescent of paranoid fear clicking on in each eye. He glanced at his shoes and shuffled before the blast of need that gusted suddenly from Miss McGuffin towards him.

Miss McGuffin gathered into her boney arms the sacks of sugar and chocolate, the jars of instant coffee and heady cheese and boxes of cookies that made up Hiram's list of staple foods, and piled them on the counter, leaning over slightly and hoping that something surely would be hanging forward inside her high-necked dress to attract Hiram's eyes, which twitched erratically around the room.

As she moved closer to him, he felt that though his upper body and head were struggling to get away from her, repelled by the violence of her need, the lower parts were slowly but irresistibly drawn towards that very need, responding with a prurience of their own, a prurience he hadn't felt since that evening five years before in 1962 when he crouched in the front of his squad car with a twenty-eight-page comic book in a place called Eden Park in the far Midwest. His eyes slowly rose from the floor, and when they stopped they were fixed forever on the interlocking shuffled maze of Miss McGuffin's incredible skeleton.

74

Elmo's sudden affluence propelled him into a class of beings he had never considered before. He had a lucrative job and a raise that had been warmly recommended to his boss by Andrew Winkler, who had also provided him with a half-interest in a Kernel Korn's Drive-In Restaurant and a vaguely defined consulting job for the Kernel Korn's chain. So Elmo left the silent majority for the middle class, where he acquired a whole new set of responsibilities.

Now he sat with his brother Edward in the Kernel Korn's in which he had an interest. Thirty yards away the traffic roared up and down the Louisa May Alcott Freeway, and ten yards away in the parking lot sat his brand-new 1974 lavender Chevrolet Sting Ray with four hundred and thirty-five horsepower, a piece of staggering nonchalance in the waning days of an energy crisis.

'Well, Ed,' he said, staring down ruminatingly at his Double Whammy – two corn fritters with a layer of grits in between, smothered in lettuce and Special Sauce, 'I seem to have fallen into a bit of luck and the living is very good. Damn good, in fact.'

'I don't understand how you did it, Elmo. You were just out of the army with a sergeant's pension and the usual benefits, ready to coast on through the years until retirement with maybe a civil service job, and now all of a sudden, only a few months later, you're driving a Sting Ray and living in a fancy neighbourhood. You sure must have hit a lucky streak.' Ed's voice glistened with admiration and envy.

'Listen, Ed. What say we get us a couple of broads and play some strip poker tonight. There's lots of swell ladies living around the neighbourhood. My boss's nephew lives just a couple of doors away and *his* wife looks to be pretty hungry. Might be a couple of the husbands away on business trips or something. We could take a stroll and talk to a few, see if we can find some action. How about it?'

Elmo stared at his sandwich, turning it over in his hands.

Then with a look of distaste that ran his eyebrows together and displayed a set of teeth regularly spaced but rather far apart, he bit ferociously into his Double Whammy. His brows knitted furiously as he chewed.

'Well, I don't know, Elmo. I admit to being a bit nervous around your house. All those swell people. Most of them belong to the country club, you know. Where I work.' Ed stared with mild disgust at the thin trickle of Special Sauce weaving its solitary way through the stubble on Elmo's chin.

'Well, fuck it, Ed, let's go for a ride in my new goddam muscle car. Blow off the swells in their air-conditioned see-dans.'

Elmo chomped the last savoury crumbs of fritter, grit, Sauce and bun, wiped his lips carelessly with a crumpled paper napkin and threw it on the table. 'Come on. Let's go.'

'OK.'

'Put it on my tab,' he shouted to the pimpled teenager in the yellow-and-green-striped Kernel Korn's uniform behind the stainless steel counter.

'Sure thing, Mr Laurel.'

They walked out to Elmo's new car and levered themselves inside.

'Brand-new,' shouted Elmo as the engine roared into life. 'Fibre glass body. *Four hundred* and *thirty-five horse*power,' he screamed as he slammed the car into gear and with an agonized prolonged screeching laid down two parallel black tracks all the way up the on ramp and into the torrent of traffic on the Louisa May Alcott Freeway.

75

McDonald Crisp was on the last leg of the annual pack trip he took, the trip that each year earned him his eighty-five-thousand-dollar salary from Hollinday Industrial Pharmaceuticals Inc.

He had driven his dog sled across the northern edge of Klinaklini Glacier, where he had been forced to wait out the late winter snowstorm tentatively nibbling at western British Columbia when he had taken delivery of the sacks from the Russian sub. He and his dogs huddled together for warmth, and he shared his tinned rations with them. He laid out the two hundred-pound sacks of uncut opium and spread his furs over them. Then he slept, with his dogs mumbling and yelping beside him.

The morning broke clear and cold. To the south Fang Peak sneered into the frozen air like a dentist's nightmare. Mac mushed on until he was just north of Tatlayoko Lake, where he left the dogs and sled with their owner, an old trapper who lived by himself in a rough log cabin. He loaded the two sacks in the back of the Land-Rover waiting for him and drove across the snow to Provincial Route 20. He spent several weeks driving, seemingly at random, across the province, camping nights, doing a bit of hunting, talking to no one.

Finally, on 16th June, the same day Eggs Freebnik showed up in Little America and tried to sell Orville a copy of *The Jesus Connection*, Mac drove the Land-Rover into a metal shed beside a mowed grass field in south-eastern British Columbia, where he winterized it and put it up on blocks. He carried the two bags outside and locked the shed.

Behind the shed, its cockpit windows and cowling carefully covered with canvas and tied down tightly to rings set in the ground, was a 1974 Cessna 210, the identification numbers November One Niner Seven Six in black letters against the leaf-green fuselage. Mac loaded the two sacks of opium, the value of which had by now risen to seven million dollars on the street but was virtually priceless when added to the Special Sauce, into the cargo bay of the Cessna and lashed them down with canvas webbing.

It was early evening when he finished, so he camped beside the shed. He was up before dawn, and as soon as it was light enough to see the grass of the field and make out the silhouettes of the trees beyond, he preflighted the aeroplane, added oil, topped off the tanks from the drum of aviation fuel he had flown up with him when he came to Canada, climbed in, and fastened his seat belt.

Before starting the engine he looked back one last time at the two innocuous Gold Medal flour sacks to make sure they were securely lashed down. Then he primed the engine and, cracking the throttle a bit, twisted on the starter. In spite of being tied down for three months behind the shed in the harsh Canadian spring, the plane started on the first try.

There was no wind, so Mac taxied to the north end of the

131

field, and with the brake held on and twenty degrees of flaps, he pushed the throttle all the way in. When the engine was up to speed he popped off the brake, and the plane slowly gathered momentum as it bumped across the grass. He held the yoke all the way back and was off the ground in three hundred yards. He eased it off a bit to gain air speed and pulled up sharply just before reaching the trees. He levelled off at three hundred feet and maintained a heading due south.

When he judged he was about twenty miles north of the United States border he let the plane down until it flew just above the treetops. Then he threaded his way through every slight valley or depression in the geology of the area until he was well inside Montana and headed south-east towards Squash.

He crossed Interstate 90 at seven thousand feet and began to relax; in his head a half-dozen unspeakably carnal starlets began to take off their clothes.

76

Orville grabbed the hose from Slim, still spurting hi-test all over the silver Coupe de Ville, and propelled him gently out of the way. As he inserted the hose into the tank of Senior's car, he said, 'My God, Dad. We weren't expecting you for another couple of days.'

'Ah, yes, Orville, my boy,' said Senior, edging out of the driver's side and over towards his son, effectively blocking Orville's view inside the car; so he didn't see that someone slipped out the passenger side of the car and walked past the Li'l Injun office to the rest-rooms on the side, although Eggs, who was leaning against the frame of the open door, did notice.

'Came out a few days early, true,' Senior continued with a glance over his shoulder to check that his passenger was out of sight. 'Just had to get away. The weather at home was awful, hot and muggy, you know how it gets in the summer. I sure hope you can clean that gasoline off my car before it eats all the paint.'

'Of course, Dad. Why don't we service the car for you since you're here? You can walk on over to the Sleepy Time Motel and get a room and we'll have your car ready for you in the morning.'

'A fine idea, boy,' said Senior, and Orville almost reached up to tug at his forelock and say 'Yassah.' Instead he told Slim to open the garage door, and when it was up and Senior had wandered off towards the motel, he drove the car on to the lift rack and closed the door again. When he got back outside there was no sign of Senior. Orville smiled.

'Slim,' he said, 'You can go on home. No, listen Slim, you go sleep on Chuckie's porch tonight, OK? Go over to Chuckie's. Understand? There's someone with Juanita tonight, so go stay with Chuckie.'

'OK, Orville,' said Slim, turning away, his right arm still bent stiffly in front as if he were elbowing his way through the swinging doors of a western saloon. Orville stood a moment in the rotating yellow light of the Li'l Injun sign watching Slim appear and disappear through pools of light as he stumped slowly west towards Chuckie Chipwood's ramshackle frame cottage on the edge of Little America, where Chuckie would be sitting on the porch with his transistor radio pressed against his ear, participating electronically in the ritual bloodless combat of his culture. The evening was warm and filled with the cheerful ceaseless song of crickets and the eternal background hiss, crackle and pop of neon.

'Where are you going to put the bomb?' Eggs inquired when Orville finally walked into the office.

'Under the spare tyre. It should fit nicely.' Orville pushed aside an electronic engine analyser and lifted a metal trap-door. From the recess he pulled out a metal box about twelve inches long, eight inches wide and five inches high.

'That's it?' asked Eggs, incredulous.

'That's it,' said Orville. He opened the trunk and removed the spare tyre. The box did indeed fit neatly into the opening. He took it out and carried it over to the workbench. The mechanic's dolly on to which he had only an hour before loaded the uranium from Owen's truck had been shoved under the bench. As he busied himself finishing the bomb, Eggs wandered around the Coupe de Ville whistling to himself.

'What are you using for a trigger?' he asked a few minutes later.

'Thermite.'

'Ah. Are you sure that will work? I mean, I never heard of

133

using thermite as a trigger before.'

'Of course it will work,' said Orville, tightening the lid back on to the bomb. 'Listen, I've bombed or otherwise sabotaged my father's car six times in the past fifteen years. This is the seventh time, so it's bound to be the lucky time. This time he'll have to know what's happening to him.'

'This bomb has just got to work.' He said it to himself as he lowered the now-completed bomb into the opening under the spare. He replaced the tyre and closed the trunk. 'Now,' he said, flipping on the hydraulic lift, 'let's service this mother.'

77

Andrew Winkler's softening hips rhythmically pumped pleasure into Flora's gyrating pelvis and the leather sofa under them grew slick with sweat. He kept murmuring 'son of a bitch' softly under his breath, and Flora, staring at the beige ceiling of Andrew's office bathroom, would answer, 'Yes, Andrew. Oh, yes.'

Senior had left that morning for his hunting lodge in Idaho, and Flora was spending the entire day with Andrew. It was something they anticipated every year when Senior went to Idaho, and this, their fourteenth consecutive year, was no exception.

The slickness of the leather increased, and Flora began to slide up and down on it with each of Andrew's mighty thrusts. Suddenly, with a snorting yelp, his nose lifted into the air and he pounded home so hard they almost slid sideways off the couch.

They lay there drying and cooling, Flora's slightly mottled thighs gently pooled over Andrew's pale, black-haired legs. Finally, with a sticky pop, he rolled off her and on to his back.

'I've been thinking,' he said in a quiet voice.

Flora's breath was slowing to normal, so her wonderful breasts were heaving less frantically. They stared away to the side, wall-eyed. She rolled over on to her side, so that the two of them seemed to be looking at Andrew, and she encouraged him with her hazel eyes.

'I have to tell you,' he continued after a moment. 'For the past two years I have been blackmailed by an employee of your husband's. It seems he saw us that evening at Owen's wedding reception in the downstairs dining-room. He recognized me when I visited the plant one day. In fact, he called up one time when you were here.'

'I think I remember that day,' she said.

'Well, I've been thinking. Now my wife . . .' He stopped.

'Yes. Babs. Your wife,' said Flora.

'You know something,' said Andrew, suddenly rolling on his side and looking at Flora. 'I haven't seen my wife in over a year. I never noticed. I think she moved to Florida. In fact . . .' He jumped up and trotted into the office, his white buttocks jogging up and down as they receded. He rummaged on his desk. 'Yeah, here it is,' he shouted.

He jogged back with a letter in his hand, his limp member wagging back and forth like a happy puppy's tail. 'My wife has a lawyer. She wants a divorce. Right here in this letter. Seems she met the captain of a yacht or something. I hardly noticed it before. Yes.'

He dropped to his knees beside Flora. 'Why don't you ask Senior for a divorce,' he said. '*I'll* get a divorce. *You* get a divorce. We could get married, and I could tell this Laurel fellow to go hang; he'd have no excuse to blackmail me any more. I've only been paying him to keep it all from Senior. I didn't want to lose you.'

Andrew's member was hanging only a couple of feet away from Flora's eyes. She stared at it as though in a trance. 'Of course, Andrew. Anything you say.' Her hand twitched once and started to climb slowly up his thigh towards the heavy jewel that winked between his legs.

'What?' he asked, startled. He looked down and saw Flora squeezing his hardening pulp with little rhythmic pulses of her hand, and he noticed that her nails were lacquered an ancient Chinese red.

'Son of a bitch,' he said quietly as Flora scooted her head over to envelop his ivory arrow in the dense target of her mouth, and he lowered his magnificent nose once more towards the tumult of musk where her legs came together.

78

Senior's palms left damp trails across the back of Margot's dress as they crawled to the zipper at the nape of her neck. They still stood, slightly off-balance, by her front door, and his head was ringing with confusion and desire, though the sharp gong in his forehead had receded to a dull hum, a kind of mental white noise that blurred all thought. His hands, however, had disconnected themselves from his conscious control and were operating quite independently, keeping in touch only through the hotline to the zinging in his silk underwear.

He and Margot floated and bumped across the foyer, fused together in a kiss that threatened to become a permanent weld of their lower faces, and began to drift unevenly up the carpeted stairs. Senior's right hand reached the zipper and with infinite patience, step by languid step, pried the small metal flap away from Margot's back and inched it downward. At the landing he had moved it three inches, and the flaps of her dress peeled away from her small-boned spine. By the top of the stairs the zipper was to her waist, where a belt prevented further progress. In Senior's head and before his eyes hundreds of tiny lights winked and flared and in his ears the white hydrogen background noise of the universal dial tone roared through the absolute zero of interstellar space, while his body sang the glorious anthem of testosterone, the mindless hymn of hormones.

As they wafted down the hallway towards Margot's bedroom with its king-sized bed and its decorater bedspread, Senior's hands tried to find a way past the belt, but their two bodies joined at the mouths prevented him from slipping his left hand between them to the buckle, so his right hand crawled into her dress and scuttled for the hooks of her bra. His thermotropic left tried to squeeze under the belt to the top of her panties and the warm crease between her buttocks. Three fingers wedged themselves under the belt and his right forefinger was just working its way between two of the bra hooks when they crashed into the closed bedroom door.

Though their teeth cracked together and a sharp pain seared

through Senior's hooked right hand, Margot groped for the door without breaking the kiss, and when at last it flew open they waltzed one-two-three one-two-three right through and on to the cool blue and silver bedspread in the dark room with the shaft of hall light splashed across it like the roar of surf. Margot's hands began to flutter up and down Senior's back, a pair of early spring robins looking and pecking into moist earth for worms, while in her head nightingales warbled liquidly in the Spanish moss and down by the river those old banjos were astrummin' and the darkies were asingin' in soft harmonic voices with just that hint of savage rhythm to send her blood flowing a bit faster, nourished by a thousand cheap romantic novels. She waltzed on and on in the candlelight of the deep plantation night and her daddy danced with her. Together she and Senior moved one-two-three around the bed and Margot visualized the room filled with dancing couples, the men dressed in uniforms of blue and crimson and gold with *Gone With the Wind* sabres by their sides and the girls with flowers in their hair swinging their wide skirts high with each waltzing twirl, and she melted closer into her daddy's safe and loving patriarchal arms.

Finally the intense suction of the kiss gave way and they drew wetly apart. Senior's hands gave up on Margot's clothes and fumbled hurriedly with his own, flinging away his glasses, ripping off his suit coat, his tie, his shirt, his pants, until, with his striped silk underwear tented in front of him, he looked up to see Margot, still completely dressed with only the back of her dress flapped open like a patient in for exploratory surgery, dancing solemnly around the room by herself, her eyes closed dreamily and her head resting gently on her invisible daddy's shoulder.

79

Unbeknown to Hiram, the most sophisticated array of electronic security precautions surrounded the Hollinday Enterprises Fission Division Methane-Cooled Slow-Burn Breeder Reactor known to the state of the art. There were microwave personnel detectors. There were human-mass infrared heat detectors. There were subminiature solid-state radar proximity alarms. Buried in the ground were sonic motion detectors to sense the footfalls of intruders. There were trip wires and contact alarms. The entire countryside surrounding the plant was irradiated by seventeen different bands of the electromagnetic spectrum in various pulses, frequencies and intensities. Anything with a brain more complex than a snail had better stay clear.

People stayed away out of indifference. The alarms never went off in the state highway patrol office twenty miles away, nor in the county sheriff's office, and gradually even the memory that those alarms existed had rusted through disuse; the lines connecting the alarms had also rusted away. Only the alarm next to the phone in Hiram's office/bedroom still worked, but it only seemed to go off when Hiram wasn't around.

He and Miss McGuffin had found a place to meet, away from prying small-town eyes. Off County Road 314 a small dirt track twisted through the fir trees towards the fence that surrounded the reactor. At the end of the track a small clearing cut into the mass of forest like a cyst. Although Hiram was supposed to be in his office protecting the plant from hostile intruders, he figured that since he could see the place from this clearing, and since no one came to the plant anyway, this glade, filled as it was with sweet summer grasses, was both a secure look-out and ideal trysting place. The alarms of course rang like crazy as long as they were there but stopped when he returned home.

It took Miss McGuffin and Hiram three years of circling ever closer around each other's flame to finally make contact in an embrace, and another two years for the intervening clothes to be removed so that all along their skinny lengths skin contacted skin; it wasn't until the summer of 1972 that their weekly summer picnics in the glade produced anything like sexual intercourse. After that, of course, it became routine, and now the two of them sat coyly naked on a blanket amid the litter of a bread and cheese picnic, their bodies radiated by seventeen different brands of electromagnetic waves humming in compact silence, planning their Fourth of July picnic/orgy here in the glade, while back in Hiram's office the alarms clanged and clamoured to his empty cot and chair.

'Should we have fireworks?' asked Miss McGuffin, her flat and bony chest glistening lightly with languorous sweat dappled with small crumbs of Wonder Bread and Velveeta cheese.

'After all,' she continued, 'it will be the Fourth of July.' The sharp vertebrae tinkled and clicked together as she laughed.

'Sure we should,' said Hiram, thinking ahead to next week's sex now that this week's was over. His imagination had been fine-tuned by his years of close attention to the seven comic books he'd been given so long ago, but he had been unable so far to figure out how to put what he had learned into practice: Miss McGuffin was shy, and he wasn't as limber as he once had been.

'Hiram,' Miss McGuffin asked, her eyelids drooping coyly over her slightly bulging eyes, 'why don't we get married?'

For a long time Hiram sat in the warm, bug-buzzing afternoon, letting the idea of marriage sink slowly through the yellowed waxy meltdown of his body, to mingle there with thoughts of fireworks on the Fourth of July and a certain sexual combination the two of them could achieve that had come to him in a moment of sudden illumination.

They were quiet, both of them, two derelict bodies abandoned by the world, in a golden globe of supreme communion.

And then Hiram, picking a piece of sweaty cheese off his chest and popping it into his mouth, said, 'Why not?'

80

The Squash Municipal Airport, a turf strip 2445 feet long and 20 feet wide, was unattended, though it had a corrugated iron shed with a gas pump inside and four agricultural planes tied down outside. The airport wavered under the same steamy sun and haze of insects that Hiram and Miss McGuffin felt at that moment. A faint breeze riffled through the unmowed grasses at the edge of the runway as a magician might idly shuffle his trick deck. A gravel road three-quarters of a mile long wound away from the airport to the highway to the north.

Nine miles to the north-east Hiram and Miss McGuffin were brushing bread crusts and pellets of cheese from each other's torso when the drone of the green Cessna 210 crossed their horizon from right to left, carefully skirting the restricted zone that protected the Hollinday Enterprises Methane-Cooled Slow-Burn Breeder Reactor.

Inside the plane Big Mac's right hand rubbed vigorously on the bulge of his crotch as his left hand rested delicately on the steering yoke, subtly controlling the plane's pitch and bank with tiny pressures. He had shortly before snorted into his left nostril four drops of amyl nitrate, which had sent such a rush of sexual electricity blasting through his frontal lobes that his autonomic nervous system had to take over complete control of the plane while he frantically pulled himself off in a blaze of bloody fantasies.

He knew, for instance, that a 1956 bright red Ford Thunderbird convertible with the top down would be waiting for him at the airport. Three incredible starlets, room-mates, with the hungriest groins in the film industry, waited in the car. All of them would angle their sopping sexes towards him and the lead part in his film, which was to be made from his first novel. He was thinking about writing in a scene in which a killer grizzly raped a woman in the woods, a powerful bear fuck before the hero killed it and got the girl.

His right hand was a blur of motion; his shallow eyes darted outside the plane, locating familiar landmarks; the pressure in his shorts built to an incredible intensity so that within seconds he blasted his sexual release into his pants just as the plane crossed the final ridge before the airport and hit a violent downdraft, sending Mac's stomach into his larynx where a complicated combination of sounds emerged, part hallucination, part sex, part surprise, part fear. Then he slumped down in his seat, his eyes rolled up almost out of sight, though his left hand continued to guide the aircraft, keeping it level with minor adjustments of the yoke.

He crossed the highway and turned to follow it, his eyes slowly unrolling as the amyl nitrate rush passed. In his mind he hacked open the bear and pulled out its guts, his hands bloodied in the sacred rite of death and initiation, and the pink-fleshed rubbery starlets slid all over him in a warm bubble bath of tits and thighs.

He pulled off the throttle and dipped the nose, lowering the Cessna to fifteen hundred feet in one great swoosh; the air speed hit a hundred and ninety knots. He levelled off, allowing the speed to bleed away. When he crossed over the airport he hit the gear and flaps, and when he turned on downwind he saw, next to the iron shed, the red Thunderbird convertible, its

140

top down, with three girls in halters and shorts craning their heads to watch him land.

Such an intense wave of sexual disgust and hatred swept through him that his hand trembled on the controls all the way down on base and on final approach, and when the plane hit the ground he botched the landing so badly that it bounced thirty feet into the air and ballooned and bobbled all the way down the runway so he had to bite his lip and dump the plane flat-legged on to the turf in the worst landing of his career; he was sure he could hear the chiming tinkle of female laughter follow him to a stop.

81

'You know your father has someone with him,' Eggs informed Orville the morning after Slim had poured gasoline all over Senior's silver Coupe de Ville.

'He has someone with him?' Orville was hunched down inside his Li'l Injun uniform, hands in his pockets, and the two of them were walking through the early July morning to breakfast.

'Yep. A girl. She got out of the car while you were gassing up your father's car.'

'A girl? My father? Senior, with a girl? Senior doesn't care about anything but money. Why would he be with a girl?'

'I don't know,' said Eggs, smoothing his beard down over the front of his plaid flannel shirt. 'Shouldn't he be with a girl?'

'Well, I mean it just doesn't sound like Senior. He never even showed an interest in Mom that I know of. Just in his business. And politics. He's very active in politics. In favour of defence spending, you know. He sold medicines of some kind to the military; he's made a lot of money out of defence spending, I think. My Uncle Wilbur made a lot of money out of defence spending, too, before his bomb shelter blew him up. Made a fortune from a little jet engine part; he made it cheap and bad and sold it high. Very lucrative, defence. And now my cousin Owen. Whew.'

'Well, maybe she was a hitchhiker or something. Shall we

141

eat at the Coffee Shoppe?'

'Sure,' said Orville. 'Yeah, you're probably right, a hitch-hiker.'

They walked in and took the first booth in the back. They didn't notice the couple in the last booth, a couple so absorbed by the silent ritual of breakfast that to look at them would have been an act of unspeakable impiety.

Eggs and Orville picked up the familiar menus, with the depiction of the Shot Heard 'Round the World on the covers, and read over the list of favourites.

'I'll have a Battle of the Alamo,' Eggs ordered. A Battle of the Alamo consisted of two little forts of link sausage with an egg fried sunnyside up inside, all covered with a tomato sauce containing chilli peppers.

'I'll take a Star-Spangled Banner,' Orville told the waitress, who wrote a *4* on her pad. A Star-Spangled Banner was two waffles together with stars of blueberries and stripes of straw-berries and whipped cream. Orville always felt he should salute it when it was set before him.

'Are you and Bobalou planning to get married?' Eggs asked when their breakfasts arrived. 'You might as well, you know.'

'Well, now, I just don't know, Eggs. The thing is, I have to finish my one last try at my father first, and if I got caught I'd probably go to jail or something, and then Bobalou would be left alone. I'd hate to do that to her. So we'll hold off for a while, I think.'

'Do you really want to kill your father?'

'Well, sure I do. I've tried often enough.'

'It just seems to me,' said Eggs, shovelling another mouthful of Alamo into his mouth, 'that you could've done it by now if you'd really wanted to.'

'Well, if this bomb doesn't work maybe I'll give it up. It's true, I don't seem to hate him as much as I used to. And I have come to Little America, and I do have my own gas pump, and Bobalou. But the bomb is already in the car and it's too late to do anything about it, so I'll just have to let it go.'

'Do you really think that bomb will work?' Eggs asked, mopping up the last of the tomato sauce with toast.

'Sure,' said Orville. 'Why not?'

At that moment the couple in the last booth got up and walked towards the door, and of course it was Senior and Margot making their first sexual odyssey to the hunting lodge in Idaho,

142

and of course Orville saw them.

'Oh, my God,' he said. 'That's cousin Owen's wife, Margot, with my father. And cousin Owen is over there right now recovering from another night with Juanita.

'And there's a bomb in the car.'

82

Senior had to cut in on Margot and her invisible father that night in her bedroom in order to attract her attention. 'Excuse me,' he said, standing there wilting in his drawers and socks. 'May I cut in?'

Margot waltzed on, her dress flapping gently like vestigal wings over her shoulder blades, blades whose fragile delicacy absorbed Senior's attention until he heard her murmur something.

'What did you say?' asked Senior in what he hoped was a patient, gentle voice.

'Oh, Daddy,' she said a bit more distinctly, dancing on through a pink candlelit haze of southern romance, 'Oh, Daddy, Daddy.'

Senior began again to rise, spurred by that special warmth in her voice that sent a tiny worm of ersatz incest turning in his belly. Perhaps, he thought, if I could once again slip into her arms and be her dad, we might waltz on into the hay.

And so, stiffly erect once more, he waited until she one-two-three-ed past him and fitted his shoulder under her tilted head and his hands around her slender back and two-three-ed just right into her silent waltz, thinking, how splendid I am to fill her daddy's shoes and all her longings like this.

Something about his bulge brought Margot back. 'Why, Senior,' she said, stopping the dance so suddenly that he one-two-three-ed on before jerking to a halt himself. 'Whatever are you doing with your clothes off like that?'

'Uh,' said Senior, wilting again in his silk stripes, feeling his emotions yo-yo down again, too, and his headache return with that sharp sinking pang the settlers on a wagon train might have felt when the ridge filled with numberless Apaches.

'Uh,' he repeated, staring at his black nylon socks and realizing

143

that he could see them clearly now that his bulge had disappeared.

Margot looked down too and she laughed a tinkling arpeggio down the harp of her larynx and Senior's spirit hit bottom. 'Oh, Senior,' she said, 'we shouldn't be here like this. I mean, you haven't any clothes on, and you look so *silly*.'

Senior's spirit sank below bottom. 'I guess I'd better go,' he mumbled, all his lust blown out by the arctic wind of shame, a wind that had been blowing forever across an icy vastness.

'But, Senior, you also look very dear,' she said, and she undid her belt and shrugged her dress to the floor, and stood for a moment in bra and panties like a perfect mound of strawberry ice-cream with two dollops of whipped cream, and in Senior's confused brain a relay clicked and he began for a weary final time to stiffen. Margot reached through the fly of his shorts, grabbed him gently and led him to the bed, where they necked and necked, and Senior groped and groaned, and when the time finally came to do it all just right, Senior withered away like the ideal state.

Margot was very understanding, but Senior certainly didn't get her to his hunting lodge in Idaho that year.

But he was a good boy, and worked hard and persevered and took her to lunch and bought her flowers and was fatherly and kind, and she agreed at last to take a trip with Senior while her husband Owen was away on business of his own, although she couldn't promise him anything, of course.

83

'Senior has gone to Idaho,' said Flora, dabbing a Kleenex at Andrew's shining nose. They were sitting naked together on the couch, their legs open to the air.

'You know,' Andrew said, leaping up and stuffing himself into his shirt, 'we should follow him. We should tell him we want to be married. We should get you a divorce. We should take a vacation together. I need a vacation. You need a vacation. Let's drive out there and tell him.'

He jogged into his office and hit the switch on his intercom.

'I'm going out of town for a couple of weeks, maybe more, on business. Cancel all my appointments. I'll call in next week and let you know when I'll be back.'

'Yes. Mr Winkler.'

'Now,' he said to Flora, jogging back into the room, his lovely tool peeking between his shirt-tails, 'let's get started. I suppose we should go by your house and get you some things. Then to my house,' he said, hopping first one foot and then the other into his underwear.

Flora smiled in amazement as she watched Andrew's flurry of activity. 'But Andrew, can you really leave your business like this?'

'Of course I can. I haven't had a vacation in years. Besides, it runs itself. People can't stay away from deep-fried corn fritters, it seems . . .' He smiled a moment. 'In fact,' he continued, sliding his hairy legs into his trousers, 'I think I might retire. Sell the business. We could move to California. Or Florida. No, not Florida, Babs is living there. Anyway, somewhere. Come on, come on, we've got to move.'

Flora started to dress, feeling a bit giddy. 'What if Senior won't give me a divorce?'

'He'll give you a divorce,' said Andrew. 'He'll do anything I tell him.'

'All right, Andrew. Whatever you say,' said Flora, sliding the soft nylon of her panties up her creamy legs to snug themselves against her well-worked crotch. Something about the sound they made as they slid put a little catch in Andrew's throat. He snugged his necktie home and picked up his suit coat.

'Come on, come on,' he said again, helping to zip up her dress. She stepped into her shoes, and they ducked out the private entrance and rang the bell for the freight elevator.

'Are you hungry?' he asked as the elevator carried them down.

'Well, I guess I am,' she answered, and they laughed. They ate at the downtown Kernel Korn's around the corner, where Andrew ordered a steak sandwich.

'Why don't you have a Double Whammy?' Flora asked.

'I never eat the damn things. Frankly, I can't stand the Special Sauce,' said Andrew, almost telling her the truth. So Flora had a steak sandwich too, and they gobbled together with a monumental mutual hunger.

'Now I figure,' said Andrew, 'that we can drive tonight all the way to Peru, Illinois, where we can spend the night together

145

at the Peru Motor Lodge. They have excellent food there in the Machu Picchu Room, I understand. We can make it to Idaho in three days if we drive hard. You do know where this hunting lodge of his is, don't you?'

'I've never been there, but it's near the town of Squash, and I suppose we could ask someone when we get there.'

'That's good enough for me,' said Andrew, and they left in a dazzle of love and climbed together into the great soft cushions of Andrew's 1976 Lincoln Continental Mark IV front seat and drove smoothly off to a future where their destinies were tightly glued together.

84

'That's good enough for me,' said Debbie, tossing the Thunderbird keys to McDonald Crisp, noted novelist. He noticed that her halter top did not conceal the seeds of some of his fantasies, though at the moment there were no twinges of response in his pants. Later, later, he was thinking. Time enough. Now business.

'Help me carry this flour to the car,' he said to Doris, and he opened the trunk so the two of them could flop the two one-hundred-pound Gold Medal flour sacks into it, and as each bag fell a small puff of white dust blew up – enough to addict a town the size of Squash.

Dawn was staring at Mac's trousers. He looked down. 'Oh, that,' he said. 'I spilled my coffee in the plane.' He threw his knapsack and sleeping bag in the trunk after the flour sacks, and the four of them blasted off, Big Mac at the wheel.

They pulled up at the Hay There Ranch house in a cloud of dust, and Debbie, Doris and Dawn squealed and giggled and piled out of the car in a tangle of bare midriffs and flashing thighs, and Mac felt little shivers somewhere inside his torso for what was to come.

'Well, girls,' he said when they had all trooped through the door under the antlers. He fished through his knapsack and pulled a small metal can and a tiny spoon out of it. He dipped the spoon into the can and hauled some of the white powder into each nostril. Within minutes he was snoring loudly on the couch.

It was late afternoon when he woke up. His eyes felt as if Halloween pranksters had soaped them with slogans, his mouth tasted of compost, his throat was filled with sewage. He shed his clothes and showered, then wandered out into the warm gold of late June in his shorts and found the girls, naked and brown, lying in a provocative heap on a hayrick, baking like three perfect potatoes in the Idaho sun.

They waved him over to the hay, pulled his shorts off him, and rolled their luscious young animal bodies over his starchy flesh, grinding stalks of hay straw into him with small stabs of tender pain, and he felt nothing but mild discomfort and irritable twinges of annoyance.

'Wait here, girls,' he said, and went back inside to snort some more. His nose went numb, and he was lifted from the floor by the helium in his head. By exhaling, he steered himself over to the gun rack, and taking his shotgun he drifted out into the five o'clock shadows to bag himself a bird or two.

The girls got blankets and squirmed down together in the hay, huddled in the twilight for warmth, as distant gunfire flickered on their horizon. The night grew colder and the stars came out, and finally Mac returned, reeking of blood and feathers.

'Dinner,' he mumbled, stupified, although he had shot two owls out of their trees and there was little left to eat. But he had a hard-on, and he used it on the three smooth starlets, all faceless in the dark under an enormous white blaze of stars, with the passionless skill of a surgeon, and he fell at last into a sticky sleep that held him together until dawn.

85

It was all on the first of July when Senior and Margot finished breakfast in the Coffee Shoppe and Andrew and Flora, a day behind, finished their breakfast in the Machu Picchu Room in Peru, Illinois. Orville dashed from the back door of the Coffee Shoppe and raced for the Li'l Injun station, leaving his old army buddy Eggs Freebnik with the bill.

Orville worried, my God, Owen will show up from Juanita's reeking of sex and Margot's travelling with my father and there's a bomb in the goddam car and they're all headed this way.

Slim was standing in front of the office, his arm arced in front of him as if he were raking in the chips after a winning poker hand, and Orville almost knocked him down. He raced on into the garage and flung open the trunk of the silver Coupe de Ville, while Slim, spun once around by Orville's rush, slowly gathered a look of puzzlement on his face. Orville glanced out the garage window and saw Senior sauntering with a jaunty stride towards the station. He was whistling a peppy tune.

'Damn,' said Orville, his fingers fumbling at the spare tyre, catching in his haste the big wing nut that held the tyre down. Finally he pried it up and saw his bomb, wedged tightly in place, the lid screwed firmly down. He hurled himself to the workbench and grabbed a screwdriver. Senior, he observed through the window, was almost to the pumps. He unscrewed the lid of the bomb and had time only to disconnect the timing mechanism before Senior's voice reached him from the office. 'Good morning, Orville,' he greeted in a tone that made them pals forever; it was a voice that radiated confidence, success, pride, warmth, good humour, satisfaction, pleasure, virility and moral strength. It filled Orville with despair.

'Oh, hi, Dad. I was just checking your spare tyre. It seems to be all right.' He twisted the wing nut down and hoped the bomb would not be found before he could think of some way to remove it from the trunk.

'It's all gassed up and ready to go,' he said, slamming down the trunk lid and handing Senior the keys. 'Uh, where you off to?'

'Well, Orville,' Senior answered, his voice like fresh Vermont maple syrup pouring over a stack of aunt Jemima buttermilk pancakes, 'we, I mean I, am off to the lodge for a week or two of hunting, you know. A little R and R, just like every year.'

'Oh, yes, of course. The lodge. Well, have a nice trip,' said Orville, holding open the driver's door, hearing in his head cousin Owen's footsteps fast approaching, and trying to hurry Senior on and keep him there all at the same time. 'Uh, will you be coming back this way? I certainly hope so. I mean, we could have dinner or something.'

'I do suppose I will, Orville, in a couple of weeks.'

'Thank God,' said Orville, thinking of Owen's uranium

cradled in Senior's trunk and Owen's wife cradled in Senior's arms.

'How's that?' asked Senior, giving Orville a hard look.

'I said, "That's good," ' said Orville, propelling Senior into the front seat and closing the door. He watched Senior back out, then he saw Owen walking across the concrete towards him as Senior pulled away from the station. Orville watched the car stop two blocks away to pick up a gorgeous lady of thirty or so standing at the kerb beside a suitcase as though hitching a ride.

'Hi, Orville,' Owen said behind him, distracting him from the dwindling silver dot of Senior's car.

'Oh, hi, Owen. How was it?' asked Orville, turning away with mingled apprehension and relief.

'Just like last year,' Owen replied with a boyish grin that fell just short of being a giggle. 'I mean. Jesus. It was terrific!'

86

'Well,' said Orville to Bobalou, 'I don't much like cousin Owen, who is a terrible asshole, and I don't like Margot either, and I don't know what Senior was doing with her in his silver Coupe de Ville, but I sure as hell hope that that bomb is properly defused and I can get it out of the car when Senior comes back through here. I mean, I don't hate Margot enough to want to blow her up with my father.'

Orville felt a fetal curl of anxiety ontogenetically recapitulating all the phylogenetic anxieties of the human race in his belly, and for consolation and metaphysical instruction he sat tilted back in his wooden chair in the Li'l Injun office reading a copy of *The Jesus Connection* that Eggs had given him. Chuckie Chipwood, a shadowy and silent partner at best, was helping Bobalou man the pumps while listening to the Pirates-Dodgers game on his pocket transistor. Every now and then Orville could hear him yell 'Out?' with an incredulous groan.

Bobalou went to the office and gently midwifed Orville's pain. 'Orville,' she said for the hundredth time, her full lips pursed into a loveknot of worry and frustrated deliverance,

149

'you disconnected the bomb, right? Nothing can make the bomb go off if it's disconnected, right? It's just a metal can in the trunk of Senior's car now, right?'

'That's right,' said Orville without conviction.

'Then what are you so worried about?'

'Maybe a little jiggle could set it off. I've never made a bomb that worked before. I mean, one time I blew all Senior's hubcaps off. And one time I blew up his distributor cap. And one time he dented Andrew Winkler's Kernel Korn's van when I drained out the brake fluid. But what if this time the bomb works too well? I think it would have worked if I hadn't disconnected it. What if it works anyway?'

'Orville, you are being a pain in the ass. If you're so worried about it maybe we should take off after them and try to retrieve the bomb somehow.'

'We can't do that. They left two hours ago. I don't even know where his lodge is in Idaho. Besides, it would look funny.'

'Look funny? Jesus, Orville, you're too much. Look funny? Your father's going to turn into a mushroom cloud and you're talking about look funny. Why don't you call your mother and ask her where the lodge is. Surely she knows.' Bobalou began to pace the Li'l Injun office. There was a tiny smudge of grease on her left cheek that Orville found enchanting.

'I already called home. There's no answer. You have a grease smudge on your left cheek, very beautiful. We'll just have to wait it out until they come back through or we hear about an unscheduled bomb test in Idaho.'

'Oh, Orville.'

Bobalou glanced outside and saw that the sun bathed all of Little America with such a splendour that even the neon couldn't compete. The sky overhead was a virginal blue of amazing clarity, broken only by the contrail of an SAC bomber on a training run to the Aleutians. General Richard 'Dick' Carter was a passenger with a twofold mission: to study the air force handling of army H-bombs, and to get in some good salmon fishing in Alaska. The plane carried a small weapon with BIG DADDY II stencilled on the side. Bobalou watched the plane crawl across the sky until only the white stripe remained to mar the otherwise faultless blue. Then she turned back to Orville.

'You've got to try not to worry so. What does it tell you to do there in *The Jesus Connection?*'

'It tells me,' said Orville, looking down at the open page in

150

front of him, 'that I've got to shoot myself full of uncut Jesus and let the High of His Love wipe out all my cares. It says that once I get addicted to Jesus I'll never need to detoxify, because once I try it I'll never need anything else. It says that Jesus is the only Dope that will Love me back.'

'Oh, Orville,' Bobalou said, and kissed him.

87

Owen rumbled on through that glorious sunshine, his semi lightly loaded, his hormones spent and gone, his mind pillowed in the springy nest of Juanita's vast bosom, a retrospective smile curving his handsome lips, his Wellington boots snug on the accelerator and clutch as he slowed through the blinking light in Squash and down County Road 314 in the late afternoon to the big gate of his Methane-Cooled Slow-Burn Breeder Reactor, which he unlocked and eased on through.

Hiram Quint was waiting for him at the door. 'Howdy, Mr Hollinday,' he said. This was the one day of the year that he wore his uniform, pressed and cleaned, so that he looked, if not snappy, then at least presentable.

'Howdy, Hiram. How's the winter been?' Owen swung down with his usual grace and stretched.

'A hard winter, Mr Hollinday, but a lovely spring and summer so far. Things couldn't be better.'

'Goodness, Hiram, that's terrific. Just terrific. You certainly seem pleased with yourself.'

'Yes, sir, Mr Hollinday. You see,' Hiram straightened up, 'I'm thinking of getting married.'

'Married. That's terrific, Hiram. And when might this event be taking place?' Before Hiram could answer Owen walked around the truck and unlocked the doors. 'Give me a hand here,' he said, while Hiram, who had been hopping around after him, had his mouth open to tell Owen about the wedding.

'Yes, sir,' he said instead, and together they carried the birdcages into the office. Owen opened the big metal door and, using the dolly, wheeled the tubular frameworks with their precious cargoes to the loading bay into the reactor itself, one

151

at a time. Each canister went through its own double doors, where it could be safely handled by mechanical arms. Owen spent the next hour pouring granular metal into the core hoppers, from which it would be shuttled automatically into the core of the reactor. There were six canisters of uranium and, unknown to Owen, two canisters of sand, just as there had been the year before; and as the grains were pushed along by little pulses of air, the sand mingled, just as it had the year before, with the fissionable metal, and slowly gummed up the works.

Finally Owen came out and closed the door behind him, the now-empty birdcages stacked neatly beside the truck. Hiram was waiting beside them, jiggling impatiently from one foot to the other.

'Uh, Mr Hollinday?' He half-raised his hand, as if he were about to ask permission to go to the bathroom.

'Yes, yes,' said Owen, feeling satisfied and expansive.

'About my marriage, sir.'

'What about it?'

'Well, we sort of scheduled it for this Sunday. You know, the Fourth of July. Miss McGuffin and I, well, we have a sort of regular thing about the Fourth. And well, I wonder if I could have the day off?'

'Of course,' Owen responded after mulling over the request. 'I was going to head back tomorrow, but that's only two days off, and it is a holiday, and there's no sense me driving in all that traffic; so why don't I just stay around here and keep an eye on things for you on Sunday? Nothing ever happens around here anyway.'

'Gosh, thanks, Mr Hollinday. Miss McGuffin and I sure do appreciate that.'

'Terrific, Hiram. Just terrific,' said Owen.

88

Senior and Margot were easing slowly up the twisting road to Senior's hunting lodge, without a licence, either hunting or marriage. The mountain behind them threw the long afternoon wedge of its shadow across the tiny valley to bisect the lodge itself, leaving both its sides bathed in honeyed light. Senior felt bathed in that honey as well, radiating as he was such genial good humour and success, while Margot beside him felt as if the silver Coupe de Ville were really, somewhere in its magic insides, a pumpkin carriage, and she about to dance till midnight with some prince or other.

Senior had finally climaxed his ten-year courtship of her the night before, and now he was pigeon-proud and strutting. He had levered her into the X-Room at the Sleepy Time Motel back in Little America and assaulted her with such a dazzling barrage of erotic stimulation – mirrors and television movies of twenty-four-inch genitals wagging and plunging and sudsy baths – that Margot had simply floated away.

They braked to a stop and Senior, ever the perfect host and lover, carried in the bags while Margot settled in an easy chair and stretched her long legs in front of her. They glowed a sunny tan in the gold-green living-room. Then Senior mixed Margot a hefty drink and mentioned that he had some business to attend to, and he closed the door of the bedroom behind him and called Big Mac on the telephone.

'If we get the business out of the way now,' he said, 'we can relax for a time. How was the trip, anyway?'

'Trip was fine,' Mac answered in a voice that sounded like a pot of boiling water full of chilli peppers, hot and nasty. 'We'll be over.' He hung up.

Senior returned to the living-room and saw Margot's legs running from mid-thigh to ankle, her kneecaps oval and gold in the shaft of sunlight that had crawled from the fireplace to the chair in the time he made the call.

He fell to his knees and placed his hands behind her left knee, lifting it slowly, flexing the leg a bit, and then began with infinite tenderness to lick her perfect patella as though it were a cone of imported Italian vanilla ice-cream. Margot's eyes drooped, and far away in the drowsy afternoon she could hear the faint beginnings of a waltz and the clatter of a proud stallion's hoofs drawing the royal carriage towards her door. Inside it the handsome prince sat straight and still, a six-and-one-half-B glass slipper in his lap.

Senior munched and slobbered on her knee, working his way around the delicate oval bone and under to nibble at the two thin tendons behind. He shifted on to his back and slid under Margot's legs between chair and hassock like a garage mechanic riding his dolly under a car and pushed his face into the hollow behind her knee, where he licked and licked and slobbered and munched and ate at the delicate pale down growing there, then nibbled down her legs to where they crossed the top of the hassock, then back up to the edge of the chair, and in his mind vast pipes of Special Sauce roared while down in his reproductive ducts the fluid roared as well.

Senior stiffened as he ate, and before him *noisettes de veau aux chanterelles* with a *purée de patisson* and a light *salade Niçoise* simmered for his hunger. He ate with appetite.

Margot heard the stallion clatter ever closer, and pull up to the front door, while the prince sat solemnly amid his chattering and foolishly giggling ladies-in-waiting, and in the air the music of the waltz grew louder.

Senior was lying on the floor under Margot's legs goggling hungrily and bulging out his pants when Big Mac and the girls came charging through the door.

Margot's eyes flew open, she saw her prince and leaped to her feet, leaving Senior's tongue wagging upwards in the air.

89

Andrew and Flora rolled sleekly under the porte-cochère of the Sleepy Time Motel in Little America and alighted in a cloud of mutual bliss. The desk clerk's radar could clearly detect X-Room candidacy condensing in that cloud, so he signed them in and rang his bell for an acned bellhop with a smile that slid into a leer. He wore a smartly tailored maroon blazer with the Sleepy Time crest proudly displayed on the pocket, into which Andrew's dollar bill disappeared. The bellhop put the key on top of the television set and left the room, gently closing the door behind him. Then he waited a moment with his ear to the door.

He was rapidly rewarded by the sounds of ripping cloth and a series of grunts and squeals. The yellow leer deepened into its nest of acne and he strode off jauntily down the corridor, whistling the theme from *A Summer Place*.

Inside the room Andrew's huge stomach bobbed up and down on the undulating water bed. He was confronted by his entire naked form in the ceiling mirror, his flag already up and snapping briskly in the breeze of Flora's breath. She too arched her hazel eyes towards the ceiling and then to the side, where an infinity of naked couples endlessly repeated their two hungry forms. It sent such a powerful jolt of electric lust through her that she leaped on to Andrew with a terrible cry and stuffed him into her sopping sex and together they surfed the water bed with fury and joy until they were beached and gasping at last in an atmosphere charged with ozone.

They bathed together and went out to dinner. 'Andrew,' she said, 'I feel like a new bride.'

'And I feel like a groom,' said Andrew.

Arms around one another, they trod the carpeted hallways to their room again, where Andrew picked up the phone and made a long-distance call.

'Elmo, you son of a bitch,' he yelled, 'you are fired. You are no longer a consultant for the Kernel Korn's restaurant chain. You will have to make of your half-franchise whatever you can. You're slime, you son of a bitch. I'm inclined to turn you in to the police, but you're not worth the effort. Flora and I are going to be married, so we will no longer need the service of your silence. So kindly fuck off.'

There was a long silence on the other end of the line, during which Andrew smiled widely and winked at Flora.

'But Mr Winkler,' Elmo said at last.

'No buts, you asshole. You're through, finished. Your career as a blackmailer is over. Ha.' Andrew slammed down the phone and turned once more to Flora, demure in her summer dress, looking down at her folded hands with a happy smile.

Andrew turned on the television, and with a crackle it warmed up to *Gidget Goes Down in Hawaii*, and the two of them, slowly this time, removed their clothes while they watched three beautiful starlets named Debbie, Doris and Dawn, all nude astraddle surfboards, blow three handsome rock-hard young surfers as they rode the waves off Waikiki, and once more the surf began to crash in the water bed.

90

The Fourth of July dawned blue and clear, a warm damp haze folding the air in the sounds of birdsong; the pines seemed to crackle with lively sap, the grass softly bent with the weight of dew straightened slowly as it dried. A squirrel bounced under the chain-link fence around the reactor and rollicked across the open stretch around the building. Inside the alarm systems whispered to one another but decided the squirrel was too small to really ring for.

Hiram Quint rose and polished his lavender teeth and gargled his lavender breath and greased his untidy hair and dressed in his Sunday best.

Under his breath he sang the theme from *High Noon*: 'Do not forsake me, Oh, my darlin', on this our weddin' day . . .' So cleaned and scoured and slicked he went outside, past the semi in which Owen snored, dreaming of breasts as big as pillows and thighs like easy chairs, and climbed into his ancient Ford and drove with a rattle and bang down the road to the gate, and through the gate to the road, and down the road to town, where Miss McGuffin waited in her pretty white frame house dressed all in white and lace, a marvel of skeletal engineering in a wedding dress.

In town the children of Squash gathered their fireworks for the evening show over at the county fairgrounds or tumbled in the dust of summer vacation behind their neat houses. The sun climbed, a cosmic Roman candle brightening the day, and it was ten o'clock when Quint arrived at Miss McGuffin's door.

'Oh, Hiram,' she said, her eyes cast down to her shoes peeking beneath her wedding dress, and she gave a sigh that made all her bones rustle stiffly against one another.

'This is it,' said Hiram, fifteen years of dirty comic books unreeling in his brain, mingled with vague thoughts of he and Miss McGuffin tending the store, blissful amid the dry goods, appliances and groceries.

Arm in arm they walked the half-block to the church, where all the parents of all the tumbling kids waited to cheer their Miss McGuffin into matrimony at last with that nice Mr Quint who had now been around for nine whole years acourtin' her.

They were hitched without a hitch. No one stood up to protest, and Hiram didn't lose or forget the ring; Miss McGuffin found her voice when it came time to say 'I do,' and they kissed a pristine Listerine kiss and didn't miss and crush each other's nose. They walked from the church into a gentle rain of rose petals and rice and everyone went back to Miss McGuffin's house and congratulated Mr and Mrs Quint on their fine ceremony and drank a glass or two of punch. Then the new Mrs Quint loaded the picnic hamper she had prepared the day before into the back seat of Hiram's Ford and they drove off to consummate their marriage in the glade near the Hollinday Enterprises Fission Division Methane-Cooled Slow-Burn Breeder Reactor.

Owen sat in front of the building, tipped back in a wooden chair, a pair of birdwatcher's binoculars in his lap. He had eaten his sandwiches and drowsed in the Idaho sunlight, in a reverie of Juanita's sofa-body glowing in the Airstream trailer's fluorescents, and had watched birds hop along the edge of the pine forest. Once, a while before, he had seen a hawk circle for fifteen minutes and then plummet suddenly into the brush.

Far off in the wood he heard the sound of a car winding in second gear along the dirt track to the glade and at the same time noticed a movement towards the other side of the building through the trees.

He lifted his binoculars to see two horsemen pull to a stop just at the tree line and gaze across the clearing towards the reactor.

When the binoculars snapped into focus he saw that one of the horsemen was his wife, Margot, and the other was a tall, unpleasant-looking stranger. And just at that moment the alarms began to clamour inside the office.

91

The bell announced another customer at the Li'l Injun station this sunny Fourth of July, and Bobalou walked out, her round behind rolling liquidly inside her clean mechanic's uniform, the Li'l Injun insignia above her left breast bobbing with her walk, and in the office Orville gulped with love.

But he gulped with anxiety too. There had been, in the past three days, no mention anywhere of unexpected Fourth of July atomic blasts in the wilds of Idaho, but Orville continued to chew his nails. The night before he had tried eating and dope and sex in that order, but nothing had worked. He still jittered over his deadly present to Senior.

Today he tried transcendental meditation. 'Ommmmmmmm,' he hummed to himself, tearing his eyes away from Bobalou at the pumps. His eyes half-closed, he curled his hands into the proper meditation *mudra* and breathed 'Ommmmmm' into the cosmic void of his belly. Outside Bobalou pumped and washed and oiled and collected cash and credit cards, and in the office Orville recited, 'Ommmm.'

The Fourth of July was a busy day at the Li'l Injun station and Bobalou pumped a lot of gas, but finally there was a lull in the traffic, and she came back into the office to find Orville deep in meditation, though he had a look of horror on his face, and he was chanting to himself under his breath not 'Om' but 'Oh'.

'Orville!' said Bobalou, curving her full lips close to his ear. 'Orville, come back.'

She breathed warm breath into his ear, a South Pacific off-shore breeze that blew and curled gently past the auricula and through his external acoustic meatus to set his tympanum vibrating malleus to incus to stapes and the little hairs of his cochlea to tell his brain frequency and volume and bring him back from one trance to another. A little shiver of something like delight, plus a portion of desire and a sliver of fear passed through Orville, changing his 'Ohhhh' to 'Ommmmm' again and then to 'Oh, hello, Bobalou.'

Orville looked up at her, and she bent down and around and took his ear in her mouth and tongued it once. Then she stood up. 'It's nice to have you back.'

Eggs walked in with cheer and jauntiness and invited them to have lunch with him at the Silver Dollar Café, where a special Fourth of July buffet was in progress.

'Orville,' said Eggs, heaping his plate high with egg salad, deviled eggs, and thin slices of Swedish rye bread, 'I have just sent in a report for you, your first one as a uranium marshal. You have spotted some minor infractions of the rules of the Interstate Commerce Commission and the Nuclear Regulatory

158

Commission for the transport of fissionable materials which will look very good on your record. I'll show you a copy later.'

'But, Eggs,' Orville said, picking over the selection of luncheon meats and forking two slices of all-beef garlic bologna, 'there haven't even been any trucks through here since Owen's. How could I spot any infractions of the rules?'

'There's nothing to worry about, Orville, old buddy. You don't need to see real infractions. This is a government job; you just make them up. The important thing is to write good reports. I thought it best not to mention Owen's truck.'

'Ahhh, I wish you hadn't brought that up,' said Orville with a wince.

'But Orville, you mentioned Owen's truck first.'

'I did? Oh, God, the bomb in Senior's car. I'm worried sick about it. I'm afraid it'll go off somehow.'

'You are? Really?' Eggs looked at Orville, the two of them holding heaping plates of buffet food with wonderful Declaration of Independence names, while behind them Bobalou continued to pile food on her plate.

'Orville,' said Eggs, 'you really don't have to worry about that bomb. It will never work; that's all just a fantasy. You ought to know you just can't make an atomic bomb that small.'

The bologna fell off Orville's plate.

92

The morning of the Fourth Andrew slid off Flora into a day drowned in butter and syrup from the sun backlighting the colour-co-ordinated curtains of the Holiday Inn in Twin Falls, Idaho. They went out for breakfast, paid their bill, and then Andrew drove his Mark IV under the Holiday Inn marquee that read WELCOME BOWLERS and headed north, into the mountains.

The sun crawled up the blue sky to their right and over the top of the car, and in the car Flora and Andrew and the engine hummed together, a song of loving lust.

It was mid-afternoon when the Lincoln glided silently past the city limits of Squash and pulled to a stop in front of the

McGuffin General Store. Andrew got out and looked up and down the dusty streets of Squash. In one direction he could see, through the ripples of heat rising from the street, the decayed Li'l Injun station, slumped and vacant. In the other direction its competition glowed, a shining island proudly afloat on the haze of thermals. There was no one in sight in either direction.

Andrew walked slowly around the car, shading his eyes against the glare with his hand, then walked up the steps to the grey weathered porch of the general store. The building was ticking unevenly into the heat. It was cooler in the shade of the porch, and dimmer. Andrew tried the door, but it was locked. He leaned against the window and peered into the gloom within. The lights were out and the counters of dry goods and hardware stretched away into the darkness. No one was about.

To his left the yellow light blinked on and on. He trudged away from it towards the shining gas station at the edge of town. Once in direct sunlight again he began to sweat, and he envied Flora sitting in the air-conditioned Lincoln.

Tilted back in his chair asleep, his feet up on the desk, looking a bit like Henry Fonda in *My Darling Clementine* though uglier, was Albert Sommers, his acne-scarred chin rising and falling with each deep breath, a thin whistle on each exhale.

When Andrew opened the door of the station to ask him a question, he awoke with such a start that his chair fell over backwards, sending his feet in a somersault into the display case full of corroding flashlight batteries. He landed on his stomach in a rolling, bounding welter of batteries and boxes.

'Jesus Christ. Goddam it,' he said. 'You scared the holy shit out of me. What the hell you want, anyway? Jesus Christ.'

'I'm very sorry,' said Andrew, helping him up. 'I didn't mean to startle you . . .'

'Startle? Me? Jesus Christ, didn't I just say you scared the shit out of me? What's this "startle" shit? I almost wet my pants for Christ's sake, not to mention getting killed by flying batteries. Jesus Christ. Goddam it.'

'Well, there doesn't seem to be anyone around. I was wondering . . .'

'Everybody's been to the fucking wedding. Miss McGuffin got married to Hiram Quint. Anyway, it's the goddam Fourth of July, you expect a lot of people to be around on a goddam holiday? Especially on a day as hot as this? Jesus Christ, you some kind of *tourist*?' Albert brushed his knees off with sharp little stabs of his palms.

'Hiram Quint? That name is familiar.' A small puffy cumulus cloud of puzzlement passed across Andrew's face. 'Anyway, what I'm looking for is Mr Hollinday's hunting lodge. It's somewhere around here.'

'Hunting lodge?' Albert Sommers, son of one of the least successful of the acorn squash farmers in the area, was in a towering rage. His voice rose to a squeak. 'Jesus Christ. There's no hunting this time of year. This isn't the fucking hunting season, for Christ's sake. What the fuck does anyone need a hunting lodge for, for Christ's sake?'

'I think it's somewhere near a place called the Hay There Ranch. Do you know where that is?'

'Oh, sure. Why didn't you say so? That'll be Stan and Fran's old place. Belongs to some writer fellow now.' Albert was getting positively friendly. 'It's out on County Road Three-fourteen. Straight on out of town, that way. You can't miss it.'

He picked up his wooden chair and slammed it upright on the floor. Then he sat down and tilted it back, hitching his cowboy boots on to the edge of the desk.

'Jesus Christ,' he said to himself after Andrew had left. He leaned his head back and closed his eyes. 'Fucking strangers.'

93

Owen dropped the binoculars when the alarms went off behind him. He turned frantically towards the door, then changed his mind and picked up the now-cracked binoculars and stared through them at the two horses grazing quietly. At first he couldn't find his wife and the stranger, but at length he located the stranger horizontal in the grass.

He was squirming in a familiar way. Owen dropped the binoculars again and sprinted across the asphalt turnaround and the mowed grass to the chain-link fence, which he scuttled half-way up before he realized he couldn't get past the barbed wire. For a moment he paced back and forth in front of the fence like a caged panther, then he ran back to the office where the alarms still shrilled.

'Dammit; oh, dammit,' he gasped under his breath, thinking first to turn off the alarms, then changing his mind again. He sprinted down the driveway, stopped, sprinted back to the truck, realized he couldn't drive the semi into the field, that he would have to run all the way out to the gate and around the building to get to the woods where his wife was being screwed by some cowboy.

By the time he reached the gate his shirt was sticking to his smooth muscular torso and his brain was a seething mass of pudding. He'd forgotten the key to the gate and had to run back to the office for it.

Finally, twenty minutes later, gasping for breath, he threw open the gate and started jogging and stumbling along the fence, swearing 'Dammit. Oh, goddammit' under his breath, which came in ragged fits as he staggered along. He dimly heard the alarm bells clanging in the empty building, but he could not hear the ominous grating rumble coming from the bowels of the plant.

Nor could he hear from the other side of the plant, near the glade where Hiram Quint and his bride were in the process of consummating their marriage, the strange ticking sounds emanating from the trunk of a silver Cadillac Coupe de Ville as it bounced and slithered along the rutted dirt road, Senior Hollinday at the wheel in an agony of rage and hunger, searching for his beloved Margot.

Nor was he aware, as he floundered along the cyclone fence in a near-black panic somewhere between frenzy and exhaustion, that seven young campers from Camp Tomahawk's Arapaho tribe, all wearing T-shirts with the bloody hatchets on the front, were stealing single file through the primordial gloom of the ancient pine forest where the air was resonating with the rich smells of pine sap and turpentine. They were following, as silently as the Indians their little troop was named after, a horny eighteen-year-old counsellor named Barney Hugle, who as yet had no idea what a staggering vision of the American cross section awaited his charges' innocent eyes. They crept, heel-toe, heel-toe, along the needle-carpeted forest floor after Barney, who held the compass close to his eyes, and then, changing direction slightly, led them directly towards the picnic glade.

Their arrival there would coincide precisely with Senior's.

162

Owen could no longer see anything, lurching along in his blinding haze, so he didn't notice the three naked girls beautifully sprawled about the grass, sunning themselves near their tiny pile of clothes, until he tripped, jarringly, over Debbie's succulent body and fell with a heavy crash on to his face, which rested for a moment against Doris's glorious thigh.

'Wow,' she said, turning to cup Owen's face in her hands. 'He sure is handsome.'

Dawn scooted over, and the three girls clustered around him, gently slapping his face. He looked around dazedly at the three of them, labouring for breath.

'Hey,' said Debbie with tender concern. 'Are you a movie star?'

94

Andrew and Flora drove slowly through the hot, deserted streets of Squash and out on to the highway. They kept the air-conditioning on high, and Flora sat back in her seat, feet resting on the dashboard and skirt hiked up to her hips so the cold air from the vents blew between her legs.

Andrew glanced at her from time to time, and his nose would twitch.

They had no difficulty finding County Road 314 and moved through open fields and patches of pine wood. The Mark IV parted the continuous curtain of heat ripples rising from the blacktop. Flora tilted back her hydraulic seat, rested her head on the headrest, and breathed quietly. Her eyes had closed by the time the silver Coupe de Ville passed them, going the other way, and Andrew didn't notice Senior at the wheel, a set, stricken expression on his thin-lipped face, or the Cadillac turning off the blacktop on to the dirt track that disappeared into the woods. By that time the Lincoln was over a small hill and fast approaching the driveway up to Senior's hunting lodge.

'There it is, I think.' Andrew slowed almost to a stop and squinted at the small wooden sign nailed to the gatepost. 'Yes, it says HOLLINDAY. This must be Senior's place.' He stopped the car completely and the air-conditioning hummed and whispered up Flora's legs.

'Shall we?' she asked, a glinting sliver of trepidation spiking her voice now that the time had really come.

'Let's go,' said Andrew, starting the car and pulling into the driveway. They wound their way up to the lodge. There were no cars in sight, and the place had a forlorn look about it. He stopped; they got out and walked slowly up the steps and across the porch. Andrew pushed open the door, which was slightly ajar.

The place was a shambles. Empty Old Yardbird bottles were scattered around. Flora saw no fewer than three brassieres, one of them ripped in half across the front. A pair of pastel panties sagged over the lampshade beside the couch. The couch itself, and the rugs, were stained in patches by substances nameable and unnameable. Streaks of white powder that did not come from a make-up case were splattered across the floor and walls. Flora picked up a pair of Senior's striped silk undershorts, also ripped; she dropped them after seeing the name tag she had sewn into the waistband with her own hands. They fell into an overflowing ashtray.

The smell was excruciating.

'Whew,' said Andrew. 'I'm not sure we really need to ask Senior for a divorce anymore. Looks like grounds for a whole state full of divorces here.' He picked up a cup and looked down at the dried coffee in the bottom.

'Hello,' called Flora. 'Anybody home?' Her words wavered through the bedrooms and bathrooms and kitchen and back to her without reply.

'I don't think there's anyone home,' said Andrew. 'Let's go outside and look around.'

Outside there were fewer signs of the party: a rumpled towel, still wet; a rubber apron; another pair of panties, yellow this time; a vibrator in the grass. They looked around for a bit and then returned to the car. After Andrew started down the driveway, Flora began to laugh.

She laughed and laughed, then Andrew joined her, and the two of them hooted and howled down the driveway and on to the blacktop, where Andrew had to pull over, he was laughing so hard. They bubbled and seethed with laughter, and percolated and burped, and finally they just hiccupped and snorted and at last fell silent, only to glance at each other and start all over again.

Then Flora started sniffing. 'Oh, my God,' she said, her nose

164

wrinkling in disgust. 'Andrew. It smells like . . . Yech. Andrew, you didn't . . . ?'

'No, I didn't,' said Andrew, turning off the engine and opening his window.

In the silence through the open window of the Lincoln Continental they could hear, very far away, a long, enormous sound like air being slowly released from a wet balloon, an unending raspberry *fee-fie-fo-fum*, and wave after wave of nauseating methane stench rolled over them.

'Let's get out of here,' said Andrew, shutting the window and driving off in his air-conditioned Lincoln with his mistress beside him in the direction of California and the mythic West.

95

After lunch Eggs, Orville and Bobalou walked back to Orville's room, where they all sat in aluminum lawn chairs out in front in the warm July Wyoming sun. In spite of Eggs's reassurance, Orville continued to jitter.

'Eggs, are you sure that bomb won't work?'

'Of course I'm sure it won't work. Quit worrying about it, I know what I'm talking about.'

The three of them sat there for a long time, Bobalou holding Orville's hand, which sweated quietly into her palm in such an endearing way that she got a lump in her throat.

'Listen, you guys, did I ever tell you about the idea my former partner, Perry Bender, had?' Eggs was trying to distract Orville. 'It got him his job with the big company that drove us out of the frozen pizza business.'

'No,' said Bobalou, giving Orville's hand a squeeze.

'Well,' said Eggs, shifting his chair around to face Orville and Bobalou. 'Perry got loaded one night after we had declared bankruptcy on some of our left-over Rio Grande blue. We laughed ourselves sick and balled our girls and smoked some more, thinking this was probably our last really big party, since I was about to leave Houston.

'Well, I got just as loaded as Perry, and the four of us hooted and cried together. We'd had to sell our cars and houses and most of the fancy stuff we'd bought to pay off debts and so on, so all we had was this pair of loyal girls and the dope.

'So there was this lull, you know how it is, after all the sweaty sex and painful laughter and excited talk, and the four of us were sort of sitting around, nodding to ourselves and not talking, and suddenly Perry comes out with this tremendous whoop. "I've got it," he shouts. "Got what?" I say. "Get this," he says. "I go to our big competitors with one of their frozen pizzas. I tell them I have an idea and that I'll sell it to them. I tell them that if they don't buy it, there's someone else who will, that I've already had an offer for it sight unseen and that they'd better snap it up. I give them twelve hours to think it over. It's worth a try."

'And Perry told us what the idea was, and we all laughed at him until we were rolling on the floor, it was so ridiculous. But Perry went to them the next day and sold them the idea.'

Eggs fell silent for a time, nodding to himself.

'Well,' Bobalou prompted him. 'What was the idea?'

'Oh, yes. I'm glad you asked. Well, here's what Perry did. When they bit on the idea enough to pay him a fee, about five thousand dollars, I think, just to hear the idea, he assembled them, all the vice-presidents and the president and a couple of members of the board – Perry went right to the top – in the company kitchens. And Perry fried their own goddam frozen pizza, though they didn't know it was theirs, in a hot skillet with some butter, thirty seconds on a side, and gave it to them to eat. All those vice-presidents standing around gumming this steaming fried frozen pizza and going, "Mmmfg, God, delicious," and so on. "Whose pizza is this?" they asked. "Yours," said Perry. "It's delicious," they said. "Right," said Perry. 'People don't want to eat pizza in the summer, don't want to heat up their ovens in hot weather. Frozen pizzas dry out in the oven anyway. Much better to fry them."

'Well, they gave Perry a cashier's cheque for thirty-five thousand dollars then and there, and a five-year contract. "You look this contract over," they told him. "If you don't like it, OK. If you do like it, we will give you another cheque for thirty-five thousand dollars when you sign it." The contract included a five per cent share of every frozen pizza they sold with his cooking idea on the package. Perry became very rich again, and they offered him a consulting job on top of it . . .

'He sure did know the pizza business.'

'Wow,' said Bobalou, and even Orville smiled in admiration.

'You know,' said Eggs after a pause. 'I've been thinking. I like it here. This is what America really means, here in Little America. Cars. Food, Big blue skies. Free enterprise. I've been in the food business, and most of all I love eggs. It just occurred to me that I could open a small eatery here, a place to sell frozen custard. Maybe I could call it "Custard's Last Stand."''

96

Owen panted heavily amid the grass and flesh, a look of vast incredulity seeping slowly into his eyes. Around him, arranged as in *Déjeuner sur l'herbe*, the three stars of *Gidget Goes Down in Hawaii* all stared at him with expressions of mingled awe and glee. He saw, right next to his face, a pert round breast, completely tanned, no white bra marks; it was slumped coyly over so its nipple stared straight into his left eye.

Dimly he could feel someone behind him carefully unzipping his Wellington boots.

'No, uh, no,' he gasped, meaning, Leave my boots alone.

'He says he's not a movie star,' said Doris, against whose thigh he had originally fetched before being rolled over and gently slapped. He saw now beyond their faces the pale blue sky above them awash in a mist of boric acid. Who was tugging at his boot?

'Dawn, get the camera,' said Debbie in her business voice. 'We'll make some eight-by-ten glossies. I bet we can make this guy a star.' It was Debbie at his feet, now throwing his boots away and pulling at his socks.

'No. No,' he gasped again, struggling weakly, thinking that only two hundred yards away his wife was being banged by some stranger in a cowboy suit.

From his perspective Dawn suddenly towered over them all, an enormous Nikon in her hands. When she lifted it to her eye, her breasts followed her pectorals upward at her sides, so they looked at him slightly cross-eyed. He felt a dizziness coming over him. Though the sun was in his eyes and he couldn't see her head at all, he could tell she was a real blonde, and somewhere in his panicked, anxious body the testosterone levels began to rise again. 'Oh, no, no,' he moaned this time, as Doris unbuttoned one by one the buttons of his shirt, starting at the neck. Above him the Nikon gave an enormous double click.

Then, as Owen's clothes were peeled away from his still-limp body, Dawn became a blur of movement, dipping and squatting to cover every possible angle of Owen's declothing, until he was as naked as they were.

'I've got to go . . . My wife . . .' He tried to move again, but was torn as Debbie seized his stiffened root in her creative hands, and as she lowered down to plant it in her earthy mouth, Dawn was down there too, focusing in for the close-up.

While Owen was ground exceeding fine in the slowly turning mill of the three naked porno starlets, who took turns operating the camera, exchanging places with the precision of a professional ballet troupe, only two hundred yards away the long starchy muscles of Big Mac's dope-drenched body bunched and loosened rhythmically. Without the aid of his various drugs he would have been exhausted by this time. He'd had several days of Debbie, Doris and Dawn, and then the incredible party last night when he'd slipped away with Margot, leaving Senior in the middle of an impossible gymnastic with the three girls. It was only the combination of his usual amyl nitrate, cocaine, Old Yardbird and the minislaughter of a few gophers that had kept him going.

So now his body moved with a dry professionalism from which his mind was completely detached, to soar or wallow on a hallucinogenic ocean.

Under him Margot bucked and whinnied, little shrieks of 'Oh no. Oh yes. Oh my God' puffing out between each shuddering breath as Mac's long slender tool slid all the way in and all the way out, all the way in and all the way out.

On every breath Margot could haul into her lungs the smell of dead gopher blood, the smell of death that clung to Mac, and each time she did, the smell pulled the plug on an enormous drain somewhere in her groin, and a huge flood of water poured out. She came a dozen times, and when she recovered finally, she realized that Big Mac was lying on top of her still, sound asleep and snoring.

Over by the fence Owen too was finally exhausted into a dull stupor, but not before the girls had snapped one hundred and eight potential eight-by-ten glossies to help launch Owen on his new career.

97

In Little America on the Fourth of July, Slim Piggot, former saucy hip-roller and US Army reject, wandered in a fog of his own. His right arm, permanently calcified before him, though the hand could still grasp, was hanging on to the gas cap of a 1969 Mercury Montego of a faded Campbell's cream of tomato soup colour while his left hand struggled to insert the nozzle into the tank. He was partially successful in pumping gas into the bilious car, with only a minor trickle running down the side of the fender, when Chuckie Chipwood ambled over.

'Jesus, Slim,' he said after he had removed the tiny earphone from his ear and carefully tucked it into his shirt pocket. Gently, he took the nozzle from Slim and shoved it all the way into the tank. 'You can go home now, Slim,' he said in a quiet voice.

'Home?'

'Yes, Slim. Home. We're taking short shifts today. It's the Fourth of July. Understand? A holiday, Slim. Fireworks?'

'Orville, he?' Slim looked dazed.

'Orville has the afternoon off, Slim. You go home. To Juanita, understand?'

In the pink Montego a bald piano salesman from Sioux City was reading a road map. He was on his way to visit his mother, who had remarried a Mormon in Provo, Utah, the year before and had left him bereft and heartbroken. He didn't know it, but his new stepfather's family owned most of Little America.

'To Juanita. OK, Chuckie.' Slim turned slowly away.

'Good. Good-bye, Slim. Have a nice day.' Chuckie was wearing a lapel button with that slogan, but he liked to say it aloud anyway to everyone. He could say that without removing his earphone, since it expected no reply.

All over Little America the holiday traffic hummed and squealed, air brakes hissed, tourists chattered or hurried from their air-conditioned cars through the heat to the air-conditioned Coffee Shoppe. The sun crawled down the western sky, and would soon sit on the exact spot where Interstate 80 met the horizon, where it would shine directly into the eyes of the west-bound tourists, truck drivers and salesmen. Somewhere beyond that sun the Far West waited, an enormous Disneyland of camp-sites, bubble gum, Hollywood stars, and cowboys, a place where jackrabbits as big as antelopes (called jackalopes) hopped freely over the prairies and where every farmer had a beautiful daughter and an outhouse full of jokes.

The westward flow of Winnebagos over the old Oregon Trail was unending.

Slim walked, oblivious to the hooting, sweating maelstrom of traffic pulling in and pulling out, of kids screaming over melting ice-cream cones and fat angry wives screaming at thin frustrated husbands. His hips swivelled like a toreador as he walked, arm before him, through the honking, squalling crawl of traffic. On his left a radiator cap suddenly flew off and the attendant leaped back. The cap, followed by a geyser of steam, hit the roof over the pumps at the Arco station. On his right, at the Standard station, air poohed from a punctured tyre on a Dodge pick-up with a camper on the back. The owner cursed and kicked it. Gum and oil and ice-cream and cigarette stubs stuck to his shoes, but Slim walked on through it all until he reached the Airstream trailer where Juanita lived.

He opened the door and let it swing shut behind him and the noise and heat and confusion stopped. Before him Juanita loomed in pale green panties and an enormous bra, smiling her hideous, loving grin, and took Slim into her arms, fitting his stiff right arm behind her.

And then, very slowly, the two of them began to dance.

98

Elmo Laurel's only preparation for a career as a blackmailer had been twenty years in the US Army. While this ordinarily would have been enough, since it supplied him with some of the necessary skills, it did not give him the resilience needed to cope with the setback he suffered when Andrew called him.

So Elmo spent a day and a half drinking Seven and Sevens at Nick's and wondering what went wrong. He decided, in his con-fusion, that perhaps he had miscalculated somehow, not made the threat forceful or ominous enough. Something. His brother Edward sat opposite him, asleep as usual, and Elmo muttered to his quietly snoring form for several hours.

They closed Nick's on Friday night, and again on Saturday night, and opened the bar on the Fourth of July. Elmo spent enough time there that day to down twelve patriotic Seven and Sevens and devise a plan.

He drove and wove his lavender Sting Ray through the light holiday traffic on the Louisa May Alcott Freeway to the Warren G. Harding Industrial Park and the Hollinday Industrial Pharmaceuticals plant. He parked sloppily in the almost empty lot and let himself in with his key, anticipating, in his sergeant's brain, if I can't blackmail Mr Winkler at least I can sell the secret of the Special Sauce.

Elmo had received fifty-dollar bonuses on two separate occasions. Once he had submitted a suggestion that they add a relish with pickled chilli peppers to the Special Sauce. Later he had entered another suggestion that they remove the new relish.

Both suggestions had been immediately adopted.

And Elmo had exposed one industrial spy, for which he'd received a special bonus and a raise. He'd been considering exposing another spy soon but had been waiting for the right time.

However he did not know the secret of the Special Sauce, though he had loitered around the door with the electronic lock and had seen Senior use his key to open the door and go into the Mixing Room.

So now he gowned himself and stole softly through the deserted white corridors in his paper-soled shoes. On this holiday weekend there was no one around except the watchman, asleep in his tiny office, and the pipes were, for once, silent. No busy figures huddled around the stainless steel vats pouring ingredients; no mayonnaise roared through the huge conduits from room to room; no mixing and blending machines whirred.

Elmo stood swaying in front of the door with no knob, a grey iron door in the otherwise white sterility of the corridor. He then moved swiftly through the halls to the locker-room. There he broke into Senior's locker and stole the flat plastic key to the door's electronic lock. It was impregnated with magnetic markings that would unlock the special door and give Elmo the secret of the Special Sauce.

In the room he found only a hopper to receive the special ingredient and an almost empty Gold Medal flour sack.

'Flour?' he mumbled. 'He puts flour in the Special Sauce? That can't be right.'

He stuck his head into the sack and inhaled. It didn't smell like flour. He moistened a finger and tasted a bit. It certainly didn't taste like flour. He sat cross-legged on the floor and tasted the white powder again. It still didn't taste like flour.

He hardly noticed in the haze of all those Seven and Sevens the curious lightheadedness that began to lift him sweetly from the floor. Again he dipped his finger into the sack, determined to discover what this powder was. Perhaps he could even start his own company in competition with Hollinday Industrial Pharmaceuticals.

His head began to fill with helium and light. His hands floated upwards, as if he were submerged in a warm bath, and he looked at them, now sticky with white powder before his face. They were curiously shaped, the fingers longer than he remembered. He laughed, oh, boy, the world needs this stuff. He took another double fistful and licked it from his hands. No taste, but something was happening to the air in the room, now it was filled with a rosy colour in which bright golden shafts played like searchlights on opening night. Far away, but coming steadily closer he heard an enormous choir of mixed voices singing wordlessly a hymn of praise and thanksgiving, and his helium head began to float him upwards, so he stepped on to one of those golden rays of light and walked exultantly upwards into a blue and rosy heaven where the virgin mother in a gown the colour of the summer sky waited to fold him in her arms and hold him on her lap and rock him gently, oh so gently, to the sleepiest of sleepy sleeps.

99

Senior had slept in the orgy-litter until well after noon and had awakened to an empty house. Mac was gone, the three bouncing rubber starlets were gone, and most of all Margot was gone, and Senior tasted bile and fear. He stumbled out into the blast of heat in the Fourth of July afternoon and saw, forlorn, his silver Coupe de Ville, freighted down now with two hundred pounds of uncut opium in the trunk, and near it, under the spare tyre, a small atomic bomb ticking unevenly to itself.

He realized suddenly that he was naked but for one black nylon sock, and he stumbled back in to pull on his stained and rumpled pants and a shirt he would later discover belonged to Mac. He couldn't seem to get his mind to work. Margot had disappeared. Where could she be? Did he notice the rapt look she gave to Mac, his friend the novelist, but worst, his *employee*?

He drove away in a bleared and blazing fury; so intense was his combined rage and hangover that his vision dimmed and brightened with each heartbeat. He slewed off the driveway on to County Road 314 and headed towards town, then he got the impulse to try the dirt track leading off to the left. Margot was down there, he was sure of it. So he turned, unaware of the tiny troop of Tomahawk campers stealing silently through the dim, resonant forest after Counsellor Barney Hugle only four hundred yards to his left, both of them on a collision course to meet at the clearing near the plant where at that very moment Hiram Quint, failed cop and failed watchman, was preparing to insert into his new bride's clicking bony dampness the one rigid, red-capped success of his entire life.

Senior, in his blinding, pulsing wrath, did not hear the ominous *tick-tick* from the trunk of his car, where the timing mechanism of Orville's homemade bomb had at last found, in the seventeen different bands and frequencies of the electromagnetic spectrum emitted by the watchful electronic sentries of the plant just through the woods, the exact combination needed to set it humming towards climax; nor did he hear the grating, belching rumble emanating from the plant itself.

When Senior's car was half-way down the rutted road to the glade, Hiram was standing with his back to a friendly pine. Mrs Quint, née McGuffin, had her painfully knobby ankles locked together behind Hiram's neck, one knob from each ankle planted deeply into each of his ears. The former Miss McGuffin moaned like an empty house on Halloween. The nerves of her vagina were as busy as a Manhattan police dispatcher's switchboard the night a UFO landed in Central Park.

Senior roared into the glade and saw instantly the writhing couple against the tree. His car screeched to a stop, and Hiram's glistening member uncorked from his wife with a pop of surprise that let her drop, still moaning in a frenzy, at his feet, where she began scrabbling at his knees to get him back in.

Senior leaped from his car, certain Margot was being stiffed by Big Mac, and stopped, embarrassed, when it dawned on him that these people were strangers. The three of them stood staring at one another when seven prepubescent campers and one horny counsellor burst through the ring of trees into the clearing to join the tableau.

In the Methane-Cooled Slow-Burn Breeder Reactor all the sand that Orville had used to replace Owen's uranium had been working for the past year on sensitive cogs and wheels in the automated innards of the plant until, at this very moment, a series of relief valves started, one by one, to open in sequence, releasing the pressure in the pipes, so that a huge quantity of superheated methane began to blow through the plant chimney in a black, wet cloud with a truly terrible raspberry sound.

The smell was so obnoxious that even Big Mac was roused from his stupour atop Margot Hollinday's naked form. He jumped dizzily to his feet, and Margot crawled, gagging, up his pasty frame.

And over by the fence, Debbie, Doris and Dawn began screaming hysterically, and from their midst arose Owen's magnificent body, his prick now hanging as limp as the post office flag in Squash on this windless Fourth of July.

Back in the clearing on the other side of the plant, the mechanism in Senior's car ticked on to completion. With the fizzing sound of a great Roman candle that grew and grew in a swelling volume the thermite trigger of the bomb began to heat up, and before Senior's horrified eyes the trunk of his silver Coupe de Ville started, almost gently, to melt, ruining, in the intensity of its heat, one hundred kilogrammes of uncut opium for which he had paid in excess of one million dollars in cash.

100

'Custard's Last Stand?' asked Orville, incredulous. 'That's awful. Besides, there probably already is one up at Little Big Horn.'

'Now, Orville, I think it's kind of cute,' said Bobalou, getting up from her lawn chair. 'Just the thing, don't you think? To remind us all of our glorious heritage.' She laughed a silvery sprinkle of laughter and went inside.

'There, you see?' said Eggs, laughing as well. 'Everybody's doing it; it's the American way – you can think up examples yourself. They seize opportunity by the horns . . .'

'Uh,huh,' said Orville. 'The Little Big Horns.'

'Exactly,' said Eggs, smoothing his beard over the front of his light plaid shirt, as though preparing it to dry in the luxuriant afternoon sunlight. He stretched his legs in front of him and curled his toes inside his hiking boots.

The holiday sun and heat were good, and here, on the north side of Little America, they were away from the traffic and noise of the service complex, so that the distances in front of them, green with new wheat, were calm and comforting.

Bobalou returned carrying Orville's overalls and a sewing kit. She sat down again in her chair and repaired the Li'l Injun patch on the front, which was hanging from the pocket by a thread. She carefully centred the patch and stitched it up with tiny, practised movements of the needle.

The afternoon was a river with a deep current but no sign of motion; no ticking to divide the time in segments, no pressing demands of routine to intrude on the smooth and steady circulation of their breathing. Only the background hum of distant traffic against which the occasional song of a bird or rustle of some small animal in the wheat could be heard. Overhead a hawk sailed on the rising air with such epiphanal grace that Orville and Eggs, leaning back in their separate chairs, both felt as if the winds of its passage flowed over their own wings. Bobalou continued to sew her small stitches, and the little Indian became once more a part of Orville's uniform, just under his name. In her concentration a tiny furrow appeared between her eyes, and to Orville, looking away from the floating hawk at her, the furrow seemed to contain a secret message for him that was very dear and clear, though entirely wordless.

The sun moved without moving through the pale blue sky, and their shadows on the dusty ground beneath them lengthened without lengthening. Orville's breathing continued in a slow, steady rhythm, and gradually his mind began to sing an endless 'Ommmm' that flowed into his lungs and belly and out again without a seam or joint, and the troubled thoughts of bombs and death and hate that had been hideously dancing with fear and guilt in his head steadily dwindled away over a horizon that, in

175

or out of time, also disappeared, and all his time in the Little America transcendental meditation study group seemed to be paying off.

So the horror was doubled and doubled again when the phone in his room rang with a ghastly clamour that sent a lance as big as a Douglas fir crashing through his stomach, leaving acid fear and total paralysis in its wake. The bomb had exploded, radioactive death filled the air, his father was atomized along with Owen's wife, his mother a stricken widow, and the minions of the law were on his trail!

The three of them were jolted for a moment, then Bobalou put down her sewing and calmly got up. 'I'll get it,' she said, and went inside.

Orville sat stock still in his blind red haze of horror.

'Hello,' he heard Bobalou say. 'Yes. Oh, yes. Oh, my God!' And here Orville's fears gathered and leaped into his throat, and he began to shake.

'Is that so? Oh. OK, I'll tell him. Yes, indeed. Yes. Goodbye.' Bobalou signed off and hung up.

She came outside to a quaking Orville. 'Orville,' she said, with what seemed to be a tiny smile. 'That was your father, calling from someplace called Squash, Idaho. He said to tell you, and I quote, "My goddam car has *melted*." '

The three of them stood there, in the yellow sun under the blue, blue sky, for a time and a time.

And then they began to laugh.